PARTY,
I Decided to Live a Quiet Life
in the Countryside

4

ZAPPON

Illustration by
Yasumo

"Such
power..."

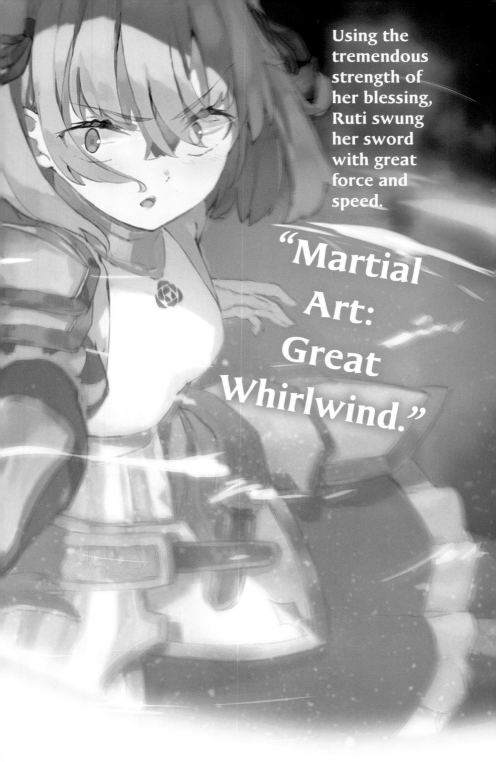

Using the tremendous strength of her blessing, Ruti swung her sword with great force and speed.

"Martial Art: Great Whirlwind."

CONTENTS

Illustration: Yasumo
Design Work: Shindousha

BANISHED FROM THE HERO'S PARTY,

I Decided to Live a Quiet Life in the Countryside

4

ZAPPON

Illustration by
Yasumo

YEN ON

New York

Banished from the Hero's Party, I Decided to Live a Quiet Life in the Countryside, Vol. 4
Zappon

Translation by Dale DeLucia
Cover art by Yasumo

▼ ▼ ▼ ▼ ▼ ▼ ▼ ▼ ▼ ▼ ▼ ▼ ▼ ▼ ▼ ▼ ▼ ▼ ▼ ▼

SHIN NO NAKAMA JYANAI TO YUUSHA NO PARTY WO OIDASARETANODE, HENKYOU DE SLOW—LIFE SURUKOTO NI SHIMASHITA Vol. 4
©Zappon, Yasumo 2019
First published in Japan in 2019 by KADOKAWA CORPORATION, Tokyo.
English translation rights arranged with KADOKAWA CORPORATION, Tokyo through TUTTLE-MORI AGENCY, INC., Tokyo.

English translation © 2021 by Yen Press, LLC

Yen On
150 West 30th Street, 19th Floor
New York, NY 10001

Visit us at yenpress.com
facebook.com/yenpress
twitter.com/yenpress
yenpress.tumblr.com
instagram.com/yenpress

First Yen On Edition: September 2021

Yen On is an imprint of Yen Press, LLC.
The Yen On name and logo are trademarks of Yen Press, LLC.

▼ ▼ ▼ ▼ ▼ ▼ ▼ ▼ ▼ ▼ ▼ ▼ ▼ ▼ ▼ ▼ ▼ ▼ ▼ ▼

Library of Congress Cataloging-in-Publication Data
Names: Zappon, author. | Yasumo, illustrator. | DeLucia, Dale, translator.
Title: Banished from the hero's party, I decided to live a quiet life in the countryside / Zappon ; illustration by Yasumo ; translation by Dale DeLucia ; cover art by Yasumo.
Other titles: Shin no nakama ja nai to yuusha no party wo oidasareta node, henkyou de slow life suru koto ni shimashita. English
Description: First Yen On edition. | New York : Yen On, 2020.
Identifiers: LCCN 2020026847 | ISBN 9781975312459 (v. 1 ; trade paperback) | ISBN 9781975312473 (v. 2 ; trade paperback) | ISBN 9781975312497 (v. 3 ; trade paperback) | ISBN 9781975312510 (v. 4 ; trade paperback)
Subjects: CYAC: Ability—Fiction. | Fantasy.
Classification: LCC PZ7.1.Z37 Ban 2020 | DDC [Fic]—dc23
LC record available at https://lccn.loc.gov/2020026847

ISBNs: 978-1-9753-1251-0 (paperback)
978-1-9753-1252-7 (ebook)

1 3 5 7 9 10 8 6 4 2

LSC-C

Printed in the United States of America

CHARACTERS

Red
(Gideon Ragnason)

Kicked out of the Hero's party, he headed to the frontier to live a slow life. One of humanity's greatest swordsmen with many feats to his name.

Rit
(Rizlet of Loggervia)

The princess of the Duchy of Loggervia. Adventured with Red's party in the past. One thing led to another, and she forced herself into Red's shop and is now living with him. An easily embarrassed girl who has outgrown her more combative phase.

Shisandan

A general in the demon lord's army who killed Rit's master. Disguised as Danan, he has gotten close to Ares. An Asura demon who holds a special position.

Ruti Ragnason

Red's younger sister and possessor of the Divine Blessing of the Hero, humanity's strongest blessing. She was extremely attached to her big brother and always clung to him when the two were younger. Before he left the party, Red used to dote on his cute little sister.

Ares Srowa

Bearer of the Divine Blessing of the Sage, greatest of the Mage blessings. The man who pushed Red out of the party. Son of a failed duke, he joined the Hero's party in order to restore his family's power.

Tisse Garland

A young girl with the Divine Blessing of the Assassin, she was brought in by Ares to replace Red. Largely expressionless but has the greatest common sense of anyone in the Hero's party. Keeps a pet spider she named Mister Crawly Wawly.

Theodora Dephilo

The pinnacle of human clerics and assistant instructor of the temple knight's style of spear wielding. Bearer of the Divine Blessing of the Crusader. A warrior at heart, she has a stoic personality. She has a high opinion of Red's abilities.

Danan LeBeau

A big, brawny man with the Divine Blessing of the Martial Artist. Used to be the master of a dojo in a town that was destroyed by the demon lord's army. Despite this, there is no trace of that dark past in his hearty personality.

Albert Leland

Zoltan's former premier adventurer. He was defeated by Red during the Devil's Blessing incident. He long dreamed of fighting alongside the Hero and is currently traveling together with Theodora, one of Ruti's companions.

Prologue

The Sage's Advent

The first time I saw *her,* my heart raced as it never had before.

In a faded, washed-out world, she shone brilliantly. I recognized as much because of who I was. She was the Hero, and I was the Sage.

I was fated to be by the Hero's side, just like those old triumphant stories.

I can still remember that moment, even now. I was working on the budget apportioning subsidies to each of the guilds in the capital. This was an important task to be sure but hardly one that could be said to be worthy of a Sage.

At the time, we were in the midst of a string of consecutive losses to the demon lord's forces, and the elite Bahamut Knights struggled to keep the front lines from collapsing. Naturally, all available resources went to funding military preparations, and subsidies to the guilds were cut to the bare minimum. Even a child could understand that much, yet the incompetent guilds schemed in every way they could, from bribes to threats, to get more for themselves.

Such hopeless fools. And I, a Sage, was pointlessly wasting my life dealing with the likes of them. It was unbearable.

"Your lordship."

I was in the middle of working on the documents to present at the budget meeting when my assistant's words interrupted me. Sighing, I set my pen down.

"What is it? If it's one of the guilds wanting a meeting, say I'm in an appointment and decline."

One could have set a clock by such visits. Even I could not begin to comprehend why those incompetents were so carefree with danger at the door.

"It's not someone from a guild, sir. Baron Ragnason, the vice-commander of the Bahamut Knights is requesting an audience."

"Baron Ragnason... Ah, the one with the odd blessing."

"Odd blessing, sir?"

I heard his inquiry, of course, but it was poor manners to probe into others' blessings. What's more, it irked me that I had to explain such basic courtesy. I gestured for my assistant to show the man in as I moved toward the parlor.

"Still, Baron Ragnason? What business would a parvenu, a mere single-generation aristocrat, have with me?"

Baron Ragnason had gained noble status as the vice-commander of the Bahamut Knights, but he was the first of his lineage to achieve anything of notoriety. He possessed no history, no inheritance. As the heir of a marquis, abasing myself with an upstart like Baron Ragnason seemed wholly unnecessary. As I waited in the parlor, mulling over such thoughts, the baron, and a blue-haired girl I had never met before, arrived.

The young woman had a melancholic expression, so my first thought was to wonder if she was a slave he had taken.

"It's an honor to meet you, Lord Srowa. I am Gideon Ragnason," he said with a smile, extending his hand.

Parvenu though he was, that did not change the fact he was a knight. There was nothing to be gained by ignoring his proffered greeting. I returned the handshake with a reluctant, polite smile.

"A pleasure, Baron Ragnason. What brings you here today?"

"I'd like to introduce my younger sister."

"Sister?"

The girl I had assumed to be a slave was apparently his sibling. I had not been aware that Baron Ragnason had any.

"I am Ruti Ragnason." The girl introduced herself with no trace of sociability on her face.

"My sister was in the countryside, so I pray you might forgive her manners," Gideon said, bowing his head to me.

Perhaps the girl might have objected, but if this was indeed his kin, why had he not introduced her on the social circuit in the capital already? Gideon did not have any heritage to speak of, but he had been entrusted as the second-in-command of the capital's elite Bahamut Knights at a young age. He was quite popular, and there were plenty of aristocrats and powerful merchants who would love to count him among the ranks of their factions. Maybe his sister was not as capable? Could it have been that she bore a problematic sort of blessing?

"The purpose of my visit is to request assistance from you, Lord Srowa, as a Sage."

"Assistance? I'm afraid I'm quite a busy man."

"I'm well aware, and I do not ask this lightly. However, I believe that this will be a matter that will allow you to provide a great service to the kingdom…something truly meritorious."

"Meritorious?"

I was annoyed with myself for instinctively fixating on that. Baron Ragnason… In the company of two Ragnasons, that manner of address would become tedious. I decided that calling the man Gideon was preferable. When I checked with him, he replied, "I don't mind at all," with a smile that radiated confidence.

"Proof is more convincing than explanation. It would be faster for you to see for yourself. Could I ask you to use Appraisal on my sister?"

"Appraisal?"

There were countless blessings in this world, but amid them all, only two had access to Appraisal—Sage and Saint. It was an incredibly useful skill that allowed the user to observe a target's blessing.

"And why exactly must I do this for you?"

"Because my younger sister's blessing is that unique."

I focused my mind and looked straight into Ruti's red eyes. And there *she* was.

"Wha—?!"

I was overwhelmed by the brilliance. *She* was beautiful and sublime. This was probably a sensation that only those with Appraisal could understand, but blessings had a form to them. Fighter, Thief, and other common blessings were dull, like pebbles at a riverbank. Higher-tier blessings like Sage and Crusader had a beautiful form to them—artisan-cut gemstones. Yet this girl's beauty... It was a heavenly radiance that could not be put into words. Nothing but a miracle could explain such an existence. Human hands could never grasp this magnificence. *Her* name was the Hero.

It was the first time in my life I had felt admiration for a Divine Blessing other than Sage.

"Lord Srowa."

Gideon called me back to reality from the allure of that blessing. I steeled myself and looked away from *her*, disengaging my Appraisal.

"...You were right. This has been quite the important encounter for me."

"Lord Srowa, I would like you to be the witness to attest to my younger sister's blessing."

"You are asking me to confirm what she is?"

"Even with testimony from one as influential as you, convincing the palace will be a trying ordeal. However, the Hero should be given whatever she needs to succeed. As such, the king must be made to accept her blessing."

"True. If she intends to fight the demon lord's forces, having an army for support is of paramount importance. A pledge from the king backing her quest would be ideal."

It was possible to probe the contents of a blessing with Sage's Appraisal. However, there was no way to demonstrate the integrity of their testimony without another Sage or Saint to corroborate.

The return of the Hero, a figure of legend. Gaining royal recognition would entail far more than my word. Doubtless, it would require convincing accomplishments.

"I see. So this is why I was granted the Sage."

"Hmm?"

"Sorry, I was just speaking to myself."

Gideon looked puzzled at my murmurings, but his thoughts mattered little to me.

"Yes, Ruti the Hero, I, Ares the Sage, shall gladly assist you."

I had finally found my reason for living. There could be no doubt that God had granted me my blessing to aid the Hero.

"I see! It's reassuring to have your support, Lord Srowa."

"Ares is fine."

This time I held out my hand.

"You have done well to guide the Hero thus far, Gideon."

"Hn?" The man furrowed his brow slightly at that, perhaps not understanding the meaning of my statement.

Gideon had fulfilled his role, and now it was my turn to do mine. I was Ares the Sage—he who, together with the Hero, would right the world.

That was the day my life truly began.

Chapter 1

- - - - - - - - -

Trampled Slow Life

In Zoltan's working-class section, Ares's eyes filled with loathing as he looked up at the RED & RIT'S APOTHECARY sign.

"Bringing the Hero to such a pathetic little shop… What are you scheming, Gideon?"

Ares and the Asura demon Shisandan, who had assumed the form of Danan, were standing in front of the humble shop.

Ares had chased Ruti halfway across the world after she'd disappeared with the airship. At last, his journey had led him here. He had been aided along the way by Albert, who had struck a deal with a contract demon to fight alongside the Hero—and Shisandan. More than anything external, however, it was Ares's obsession with Ruti's blessing that had gotten him this far.

Ruti was not there, though. She was currently with the Alchemist Godwin in the ancient elf ruins on the mountain, seeking to create the Devil's Blessing.

Red—the name Gideon had taken in Zoltan—was nowhere to be found, either. He was headed to the ruins with the real Danan to save Ruti. It went without saying that whatever scheme Ares had imagined, was false. Red would never, even in his dreams, have thought that Ruti would come to Zoltan.

Ares was fixated on the Hero but didn't understand anything about Ruti or Red.

Raising a hand, Ares touched the door. The iron lock holding the thing closed turned to dust. For a high-level Sage, it was a simple task to destroy a standard lock without making a sound, using magic.

He stepped confidently into the shop where Red and Rit lived. The place was decidedly empty. Ares searched through the entire building on the chance that there was a secret room hidden somewhere, but it was clear that no one was around.

The tableware Red and Rit had bought together, the walnut double bed Stormthunder had made, Red's notes about various illnesses that spread around Zoltan, the tools he had used to prepare remedies, the living room where everyone had shared such delicious meals, the kitchen where those dishes had been made, and the storefront where Red and Rit had sold so much medicine to the people of Zoltan...

Ares tore through it all, flipping what he could and smashing or trampling everything else. The Sage stomped around the house, stewing at the fact that he had not gained anything for his efforts.

"Dammit!"

With a knife, Ares tore into the bed to see if there was aught concealed within. Shisandan's lips curled in amusement.

"So you've turned this place upside down, and what we've learned is that there's no discovery to be made here."

"Shut your damned mouth!"

Shisandan just shrugged at Ares's menacing shout.

"It seems likely that Gideon has gone off to wherever the Hero is."

"And what evidence do you have to support that?" Ares snarled.

"Why ask me? You're the one who said the Hero came here because she realized Red was Gideon, right? If that's true, then shouldn't we assume they are working together?"

"...Hmph..."

Ares violently kicked the front door open and headed outside.

Shisandan started to follow, but paused for a moment to examine things. The medicine cupboards had been thrown open, and the substances inside scattered around the floor. The angel statue in the center of the room had been toppled, breaking one part of the wings.

It was a tragic scene. Red and Rit had shared so many smiles together in the sleepy little home. The place was a symbol of their slow life together.

"Hmm."

What would Gideon think when he saw this state of things?

"Humans are truly fascinating creatures."

The Asura demon Shisandan could feel his interest in the human species grow deeper still at the thought that Ares, who had just torn the building apart, was the very same creature who had journeyed together with Gideon for so long.

*　　　　　*　　　　　*

"Shisandan is still alive?" Red could not help repeating it back.

He and Danan were running along a road through wetlands.

"No doubt. The guy who bit my right arm off was definitely the same Asura demon we fought in Loggervia. There's no mistaking it."

"But didn't we defeat him?"

We'd quite literally seen his head roll. There hadn't been time to recover his whole corpse, but Rit had carried his skull back to Loggervia and offered it to the king as proof of taking vengeance for Gaius. I'd heard that after that, it had been left on display for a while before being buried in a grave.

"Are you sure it isn't a brother or something?" I questioned.

"No, I never forget someone I've fought before. That figure, and the way he wielded his sword, that was Shisandan for sure."

If Danan was that certain, then there was no way he was wrong.

"Hmm, there's a lot about the dark continent and demons that we still don't know... Can they revive the dead?" I wondered aloud.

"If you don't know, there's no way I would. But it's not really something to be worried about. I'll just have to keep murdering him every time he comes back. That's all. Nothing to it," Danan said with a hearty laugh.

Ahead of us, a guard was riding a horse. We dashed past on either side of it. By the time the man started calming his steed, which had reared up in shock, we were already far into the distance. Though it must have appeared a remarkable pace, I was moving slower than usual so Danan wouldn't fall behind.

"You've taken Immunity to Fatigue now, too?"

"Yeah, it's a skill in Martial Artist."

Immunity to Fatigue, something I had only reached after raising a common skill to mastery, was freely available as an inherent skill. Inherent skills really were powerful. Any average person trying to match the pace we were keeping would have been gasping for air in a matter of seconds.

"Gideon!"

"...!"

Danan and I felt a daunting presence above us. We immediately ducked into the underbrush and looked up. A dragon was flying high in the air.

"A spirit drake?" I wondered aloud.

"Someone would've had to have summoned it, then," replied Danan.

"I don't think there's anyone in Zoltan who can use magic at that high a level."

Conjuring a drake was the pinnacle of the summoning line of spells and required incredibly high-level magic. Forget Zoltan; there wasn't even anyone who could accomplish that in Central.

"That direction... Wait, isn't it headed for the mountain where you said the Hero was?"

"Yeah, it looks like it. Who's the rider?"

Moving as the crow flies as opposed to following a road that wound through the wetlands was far swifter.

"Don't worry about me, Gideon. Just go on ahead. I'll catch up as fast as I can."

"Sorry."

"Be careful. It's dangerous to assume there's nothing in the boonies that can tangle with us. The hairs on the back of my neck are standing up like they do whenever I'm about to fight someone powerful."

I touched the hilt of the bronze sword at my waist. "I'm weak, so I'm not about to make that sort of mistake," I replied. My feeble bronze sword was incapable of wrecking anything or anyone too great. "I'm just going to do what I can. If I happen upon a strong opponent, I plan to hide. So make sure you catch up quickly."

I flashed a smile and then dashed off at full speed. Before long, Danan was a point in the distance behind me. Then he vanished from sight altogether. The spirit drake in the sky remained visible all the while, however. It was incredibly fast.

"It's had its speed enhanced or something," I remarked.

Had the flying beast and I been on the same course, we would've been an even match, but I was stuck following a path on the road. Every curve and bit of mud slowed my advance.

"Ruti should be okay, though..."

My little sister was far, far stronger than me. There was probably nothing I needed to worry about. Still, the thought of some stranger coming after her set me on edge.

After I had sprinted for a while, two riding drakes came into view ahead.

"Ah, I caught up."

Even at this distance, there was no mistaking Rit from behind.

"Rit! Tisse!" I called.

"Red!"

The riding drakes squawked and peered at me in curiosity as I kept pace alongside them.

Water and wind elementals were hovering around the creatures. I didn't have any skills or magic for analyzing, but I guessed that the water ones were for alleviating exhaustion and the wind ones boosted speed. Rit had been using her magic to go even faster.

"Did you see that spirit drake in the sky, Rit?"

"Yeah. But there's no one in Zoltan capable of that. Not even the Archmage Master Mistorm from the old B-rank party."

Rit was Zoltan's strongest former adventurer and had a clear grasp of who the powerful people in town were, so if she could say that with confidence, then there was no mistaking it.

"So it's an outsider."

In addition to Danan, there was another in Zoltan with a blessing level that could match ours. Was it just a coincidence?

"Oh, right. Danan should catch up to us in a bit."

"Danan?!" Rit fired back in surprise.

Tisse's eyes opened wide in shock, too.

"You ran into him?"

"At the port, yeah. He came here looking for me."

Hearing that, Rit seemed to hesitate a little.

"I see... I'm sorry. The truth is, I encountered him a little while ago," she admitted, averting her eyes slightly.

"You did?" I asked.

"He said he had come to bring you back, but since you were living peacefully, he decided to pretend he didn't find you. He asked me not to say anything," she detailed.

Wait. Danan said that? He definitely wasn't the kind of guy to say something like that. This was the man who took being a muscle-head to a whole new level. Understanding being content with a simple existence was beyond him.

Danan would've argued something like, "If you enjoy living together, then both of you should come with us to defeat the demon lord. Two birds with one stone." That not adventuring was a crucial part of our happiness would be totally lost on him. Danan was just that sort of guy.

"When was that?" I inquired.

"Ummm, the first time I saw him in Zoltan was when I was investigating the production base for the Devil's Blessing...," responded Rit.

That didn't make sense. Danan said he'd only arrived in Zoltan today. I couldn't think of a reason for him to lie. Yet there was no reason for Rit to fib now, either.

"Rit, was there anything different about him?"

"Different? Not really? But I never spoke with him that much. So I couldn't say for sure."

When Rit joined the Hero's party and we'd ventured through the bewitching woods, Theodora and Danan had stayed behind to help defend Loggervia, so she had never gotten to know the Martial Artist.

Even so, she should have caught how out of character he had acted with her.

"Did your Danan have both arms?" I questioned.

"Eh? I don't really get what you mean..."

"I'm speaking literally. His left arm and right arm. Did he have both of them?"

"Y-yeah?"

"What are you getting at?" Tisse tilted her head, lost to what the point of my question was.

"The Danan I met was missing his right forearm," I stated.

"Mr. Danan lost an arm?! What happened?!"

"B-but when I saw him, he definitely had both limbs..."

"...Rit... It's not like I know all the details, and trying to tell you not to be surprised is pointless, but—"

"I'm already plenty shocked!"

"According to Danan, his right arm was bitten off by... Shisandan."

Rit froze. Sensing its rider's confusion, her drake tried to stop, but I reached out and pulled the reins, urging it to keep running. It looked at me, black eyes filled with unease, but it obediently continued forward.

"That's not possible! We killed that monster!"

"I know. You took his head back with you, and it was buried in Loggervia."

None despised Shisandan more than Rit. The demon had killed her master. Accepting that the target of her vengeance, a foe she had watched die, was still alive was beyond difficult.

Rit's expression contorted with abject hatred.

"Shisandan... That was the name of the Asura demon that Ms. Ruti fought in Loggervia, wasn't it?"

I nodded at Tisse's question. "I haven't confirmed it myself, but that's what Danan said."

"Are you sure he wasn't mistaken?"

"Truthfully, no. But Danan never forgets an opponent he's fought. I would say it's a credible report."

The three of us continued in silence for a time.

"Then the Danan I saw...," Rit began.

"Was most likely Shisandan. If he ate Danan's right arm, he would be able to transform into him," I finished.

There were many mysteries about Asura demons, the one species in all the world that did not have blessings. During the battle in Loggervia, Shisandan had eaten Rit's master, Gaius, the head of the royal guard; taken his form; and inserted himself into the nation's central workings. Evidently, he had employed that shape-shifting trick again.

"If I had told you sooner...I'm sure you would have been able to see through him. If you recognized the imposter, then I... I could have...then and there...," Rit fumbled clumsily.

"You would have gone to take him down," I said.

"...Yeah. I don't have any desire to continue as an adventurer, but he's a different story."

There was a clear conflict in Rit's heart. She wanted to keep running our shop and sought to treasure our simple life together. Those desires were unmistakably her true feelings. However, vengeance demanded action. Shisandan was the one who'd killed her master and deceived and slain all the royal guards, soldiers, and Loggervian adventurers who had put their faith in Rit.

"...I don't know whether *that* has anything to do with Shisandan or not, though."

Some distance ahead of us, the spirit drake was still flying through the air. It was gradually widening its lead.

"Whether Shisandan is involved in this or is still in Zoltan, we'll take him down together. We'll get vengeance for Gaius this time for sure," I declared.

"Red...but..."

"I know I said I was done with battles for the sake of the world and all that."

That was why Rit looked so pained. I had chosen to live with her over returning to the quest to save the world. She felt like she owed it to me to forget revenge and choose our life over settling things with Shisandan. And she was suffering because she couldn't bring herself to make that choice.

"If you have a reason to fight again, then I'll be there at your side. Our easy days aren't meant to keep us from what we want. That would defeat the purpose. There's no point in avoiding something if it troubles you."

"...I'm sorry..." Small tears dotted the corners of Rit's eyes. "If I see Shisandan, I'm going to return to being Rit the hero one last time." There was determination in her gaze as she glared at the spirit drake above. "Thank you. I'm okay now. You go on ahead, Red."

"Okay. Got it."

I poured more strength into my legs. The road was nearing the mountain, so the path would get worse, and my speed would fall. I wasn't going to be able to catch up to the spirit drake. With luck, I'd be able to arrive no later than ten minutes after it would, though.

"You two be careful," I cautioned.

The riding drakes were startled when I overtook them. They tried to keep up, not wanting to lose, but I was beyond the creatures in only a few moments.

"Gyaaagh!"

I could hear their disappointed screeches as I raced off ahead to where Ruti waited.

Chapter 2

- - - - - - - - -

Ruti's Selfishness

I had gone to this mountain to gather medicinal herbs so many times since coming to Zoltan that it was practically my backyard—I just came and went as I pleased. But this time, I headed to the settlement at the foot of the mountain first.

There were lodges there for adventurers, but the place was primarily used by loggers who supplied Zoltan with lumber, a crucial resource for a region smack in the middle of wetlands. With no time to spare, I passed out some quarter payril to the people who were gathered there to get some information—whether they had seen the drake, and where it had gone.

"It flew off that way," said a boy who'd be off to fell trees himself in a year or so. The direction he pointed was not toward the mountain. Instead, he indicated that the dragon had gone toward the forest at the foot of the peak.

"Thank you," I replied.

I slipped a silver into his hand and took off. According to Tisse, Ruti had left the airship in those woods.

The vessel had been locked so that no one other than Tisse would be able to pilot it, but the machine was still largely an unknown. It was possible the drake was part of an expedition sent out by the demon lord's forces to release the lock and steal the vehicle.

"The airship is dark-continent technology anyway, so it would make sense for them to know more about it than Tisse."

Now I had a choice to make. Was it best to get Ruti first or head to the forest? I was a little bit unsure but quickly decided that my first priority needed to be Ruti. Dealing with her issue was more important to me than the fate of any flying machine.

I set out for the ancient elf ruins on the mountain where the chimeras gathered.

*   *   *

"What do you think, Danan? With this fantastic airship, we can travel to the dark continent without any concern for the demon lord's blockade. Victory is that much nearer now," Ares boasted to Danan.

"It's a wondrous find, but it doesn't look like Ruti is around," the well-built man replied.

"True. Still, the airship is a significant boon. I'll raise a barrier that only we can approach. It would be a problem if this vessel was stolen. And with this, I'll know if Ruti approaches it."

Ares immediately set to preparing his spell. Despite being exhausted from continually using his magic for days on end, he had summoned a spirit drake and was now constructing a barrier large enough to encompass the entire airship.

Shisandan was genuinely impressed on that point. As expected of the Sage who'd traveled with the Hero, his magic power was beyond what even high-tier demons could muster.

But blessings don't grant knowledge or wise judgment. That is the true tragedy of this man, mused the disguised Shisandan.

Despite arriving at the mountain before Red, Ares's choice to stop for the airship meant he would reach the ruins second. That selection would prove decisive in what followed.

*　　　　*　　　　*

Heading up the peak, I entered the chimera territory. As usual, the monsters merely watched me from a distance while making a point of not getting in my way. I didn't run into anyone else who had gotten mixed up with the chimeras like that rookie adventurer from last time, so I pushed on to the ruins.

Nature had reclaimed many of the half-destroyed structures, wrapping them in vines, roots, and moss. The buildings were made of an unknown smooth, hard substance that wasn't iron or stone. I'd only ever seen it in ancient elf ruins. I'd investigated this site briefly before. Its defenses were still active, so I hadn't ventured too deep into the place, but something told me it was far more heavily protected than the ruins in Central.

During my studies, I had read a large amount of literature regarding the ancient elves. The consensus among researchers was that the many ruins each had their own distinct purposes. In a certain sense, it was an obvious point.

I had seen it for myself in the structures near the capital, where the proof of the Hero had been sealed. I doubt either Ares or Ruti had noticed it then, but that hadn't been a seal at all. The ruins had manufactured the proof of the Hero. The item that Ruti had left those ruins with had not been the one used by the Hero before her, nor was it an object from a forgotten era. It was an entirely new item that had been fabricated precisely where we'd found it, just like the one used by the Hero before Ruti had been.

There was no sign of the chimeras who typically wandered this area. Undoubtedly, Ruti had culled several of them, and they now gave this place a wide berth. Pressing onward, I came upon a door with a large hole blasted in it.

"If you had just operated the system properly, it would have opened...," I muttered.

Ruti had punched her way in. From her perspective, that was probably the most efficient strategy. Still, I couldn't help but chuckle at that sort of unsubtle method.

My little sister was by no means stupid. If she had seriously examined the door's mechanism, she would have deduced how to work it. Sadly, she had a few lazy habits.

Past the new entrance the Hero had made, there was a dark shaft. An elevator should have been there waiting for me, but...

"There really isn't anything here."

Just as Tisse had said, Ruti had destroyed it. There was no choice but to jump down.

"All right... Acrobatics mastery: Slow Fall."

I connected with my blessing and activated a skill. With it, so long as there was a wall within limb's reach, I could use it to ease my descent and safely drop from any height. I'd used the same ability to escape Bighawk's mansion.

No matter how hard I squinted, I saw only darkness below. I fished a light stick out of the pouch at my belt. The tool was a narrow, brass rod about thirty centimeters long. When I tapped the tip against the floor, there was a soft hum, and then the metal started to burn without any heat. It glowed as surely as any torch, illuminating the surroundings.

Light sticks were a cheap magic item that cost two payril and had a special spell cast on them. They were disposable illumination sources that shone for about ten hours after being ignited. Cheap as they were, though, they still cost about a hundred times more than a torch. The cost was worth it, however, as they were easy to light, wind and water couldn't extinguish them, and they wouldn't catch anything afire. Experienced adventurers kept a few of them around at all times.

I kicked the wall over and over to keep my descent slow. The glow of my light stick didn't even come close to reaching the bottom of the shaft. It's radius capped out at twenty meters. Beyond that, everything was dark.

Although I kept my fall slow and manageable, dropping into the shadows was still a nerve-racking maneuver. It felt like I had already descended several hundred meters. Finally, I caught sight of the elevator's wreckage. Picking out a place where I could land, I kicked the wall to maneuver toward my targeted spot.

"Phew."

Even with Slow Fall, leaping down from that high proved a little bit tiring. I had Resistance to Exhaustion, but things that wore at my nerves were still draining.

However, there would be time for rest later.

Light fixtures here and there around the underground structure still functioned, but for the most part, things were fairly dim. I slipped the light stick into my belt and pressed onward.

Here, the vines and other vegetation that covered the walls up above were nowhere to be found. Occasionally, I stumbled across the scattered wreckage of the ancient elf defenses that Ruti had presumably destroyed. Just carrying those back to the surface would earn more than I could make running my shop for a couple of centuries. There was no place in Zoltan that could afford to purchase such valuable items, though.

"From what Tisse said, they were producing the Devil's Blessing in the living quarters in the southwest section."

If Ruti was here, that would be the place. I pulled out a compass and checked my bearing before proceeding deeper into the ruins.

One had to wonder why the ancient elves had made such a giant building so deep underground.

As I walked, I noticed something that stood out from the various antiquities—a clay plaque on one wall.

"This isn't ancient elf script. What is it? Wood elf?"

The previous demon lord had destroyed the wood elves. Gonz

and other half-elves were said to be their descendants, having bred with humans to propagate. With their survival came the endurance of their culture. The wood elf language was still understood today.

"Hero Administration Bureau?"

What was that supposed to mean? That wood elves had gone into ancient elf ruins was a puzzle in its own right, but there being a clay sign with those words on it was a downright mystery.

"And this leads to the lodging quarters, right?"

Tisse had stated that there were beds in each room, which would mean that they were where the ancient elves had laid their heads at night. That's what I assumed anyway. It should just be living quarters in this direction. So what was the point of going out of the way to put up that sign?

"...Later. Nothing's going to come from thinking about it now."

It was more important to meet up with Ruti first. I ignored the suspicion and curiosity welling up in the back of my mind and hurried onward.

All I had to go on about where Godwin was making the medicine was a verbal description from Tisse. Finding the place amid the uniform rows of chambers was going to be difficult.

"Is it this one?"

It had taken a little bit of time. Rit and Tisse were probably already starting to head up the mountain. I slid open the oddly heavy door that was so common in ancient elf ruins.

"Whoa there."

A glass bottle came flying at me from inside. I leaped forward to dodge it. A second later, the object exploded with a *plop*. A green, adhesive goop splattered all around, but by that point, I was already pressing my sword to the Alchemist's neck.

"Y-you're that damn apothecary! Did you come to take me in?!"

"No, I didn't come here to fight."

"That's rich comin' from the guy holding a blade to my throat!"

"You threw a bomb at me. If I came here looking to fight, your head would already be rolling."

Godwin was gripping another sticky bomb. After a short staring match, he slowly lowered his hands. Matching his movements, I carefully drew my sword away from his neck.

"Where is the woman who's holding you here?"

"What, you've got business with her now? Just leave it be. You're obviously a capable fighter, but you've got no chance against her."

"I think you misunderstand. I'm an acquaintance of hers."

Godwin looked surprised.

"Connections with Rit and with her, too? Who the hell are you?"

"I'm just an apothecary. So where is she?"

"Like I'd know. Probably skulking around the ruins somewhere."

Having to search for Ruti somewhere in these ruins would be a burdensome task in its own right.

"…"

I could have just shouted her name, but I wanted to avoid that if possible. Ruti undoubtedly wasn't expecting me to show up here. If she realized that I knew about the Devil's Blessing and her breaking Godwin out of prison, she would likely be despondent. There was a chance she'd run, too. Handling this face-to-face was best. That way, I'd have the opportunity to explain myself and make it clear I wasn't angry.

"Hey, Godwin."

"What?"

"Call out for her."

"M-me?"

"If you shout, she should be able to hear you with the skills she has."

"Do it yourself. I damn sure don't trust you. If you're some Assassin and she thinks I betrayed her, what do you think happens to me?"

"Then just say I threatened to kill you if you didn't do it."

"Not happening. I don't think you understand how terrifying that girl is."

What a pain.

"Nothing I can do to convince you?" I pressed.

"Not a one."

"Don't say I didn't give you a chance, then." I grabbed Godwin's left hand, the one holding the other bomb. It was dangerous, so I wrested it away and set it gently on the floor.

"Wh-what are you doing…?"

Godwin looked nervous as he tried to pull his hand free, but I wasn't letting go.

"Don't worry, this won't cause permanent damage."

"Wh-what do you mean…? Hey! Stop it!"

Realizing my intent, Godwin started frantically trying to pull away.

"Also, my Rit had a rough time because of you."

"Th-that's water under the bridge. We're even after you damn near cut me in half!"

"No, that was remittance for Al."

Rit had gotten into a dangerous spot with a bunch of stalker demons because of one of Godwin's sticky bombs. This was just a little bit of payback for that.

"There." I locked the joints on Godwin's left arm and then pulled his arm just slightly in a direction it wasn't supposed to bend.

"Gnaaaaaaaaaaaaaaaaaaagh!!!" Unable to endure the pain, a scream welled up in the Alchemist's throat and echoed around the ruins.

*   *   *

"Dammit…"

Godwin was sitting down, rubbing his arm. He stared hateful daggers at me, but I paid that no mind. I sharpened my focus, listening for the presence that was surely approaching.

Godwin was crucial for producing Devil's Blessing. Ruti needed him. So if she'd heard that shout, then…

The door went flying through the air. A girl raced like lightning past it. Her sword thrust out from the blur—aimed straight for my neck. It was similar to the move I had pulled with Godwin before, but the speed and sharpness were of a wholly different level.

Thankfully, Ruti's weapon stopped before it met my throat.

"Big Brother?!"

The emotion that crossed her face at that moment was something that my sister, the Hero, should never have been able to feel—fear. At least, that's how it appeared to me.

∗   ∗   ∗

Ruti and I moved to another room.

Godwin was agape, unable to believe his own ears. Still, his fear of Ruti remained strong. He just did as bade when she said he could rest for a little while.

"Big Brother…why are you here?"

The chamber we were in was apparently the one she was using as her bedroom. It was a slightly larger space about two corridors away from where I'd found Godwin.

While ancient elf craftsmen were far superior to present-day ones, the room's furniture was already terribly disheveled. Ruti and Godwin had moved the trash out of their chambers and into another and were sleeping on simple folding cots. Godwin's quarters had also been stocked with alchemical tools, food, and water. Enough to be able to get by.

I had no clue about the principle behind how it worked, but the aqueducts in these ruins still functioned. Drinking water from an unknown source was cause for hesitation, but it could still be used for bathing. Outside each of their rooms was a laundry line. The simplicity of such a thing really struck a stark contrast with the ancient elves' highly sophisticated culture.

"Brother?" Ruti asked, cocking her head to one side.

"Ah, sorry. It's just been a while since I last saw a place like this. I'm still taking it all in, I guess," I replied.

"I see."

Clearly, I would have to be the one to broach the subject. "I heard the story from Tisse," I began.

Ruti's shoulders twitched. She looked down like she was trying to figure out how best to reply.

No doubt she assumed I was upset with her. Taking Devil's Blessing and breaking a criminal out of prison were things that the Ruti who had lived as the Hero all her life would never have done. It was a complete and absolute rejection of the holy church's teachings that one should live a life befitting their blessing.

"I'm sorry I was unable to help you for so long," I said, lowering my head.

"Eh?"

"I never told anyone else, but I'd been researching a way to suppress your blessing's impulses for a while." I pulled a vial out of the pouch at my waist. It was the secret wild elf medicine that I had given to Ademi during the incident with Bighawk.

"This substance can quell a blessing's urges, too. It temporarily lowers your level when imbibed. Sadly, it's classified as a poison, so I don't think it will work in your case."

"Why?" Ruti asked, bewildered. "Why were you always trying to save the world? You were always striving to get stronger even when we were little. After joining the knights, you helped so many people. Then you joined me on my journey to defeat the demon lord. That hopeless quest, constantly fighting the demon lord's armies, traveling all over with only a handful of people. It's not like you were driven to help people like I was, but you still fought."

"...Yeah, I never did fully explain myself to you."

Ruti's chosen quest—vanquishing the demon lord.

I had been there at the outset, when a raiding force attacked our hometown, and Ruti had tried to stand against all those orcs by herself. From there, many people had joined her group for a time, but from the very beginning up until the battle with Desmond of the Earth, I had always been at her side.

Through it all, I had been conflicted about whether to explain how I felt. And in the end, I never had. Even if my intentions were good, I couldn't risk hurting Ruti. I was afraid that if Ruti knew my reason for fighting, she might feel responsible for my choices.

"Why did you want to defeat the demon lord, Big Brother?" She was looking straight at me, her pretty eyes filled with anxiety.

"I just wanted to protect you."

Ruti's eyes widened ever so slightly. Her gaze twitched faintly.

"That's why you battled monsters when we were little?"

"I joined the Bahamut Knights for the same purpose. I wanted the strength to be able to protect you when you set out on your journey."

"Why? Because I'm the Hero?"

"Don't be silly. It's because you're important to me, Ruti. You were bound to leave home eventually. I wanted to prepare myself for whenever that day arrived. If you decide to quit being the Hero, I won't mind, and I won't blame you."

Honestly, I'd be lying if I said I wasn't a little unsure. As someone who had traveled together with the Hero for so long, I had an intimate familiarity with the war's progression.

Without Ruti, the demon lord's forces would wreak significantly more havoc. It was entirely possible that Avalon would be destroyed. Such was the price of allowing Ruti to forgo her duty. Yet even if it came to that, I would remain her ally. That was the decision I had made.

"Are... Are you sure? I left all my comrades behind. I broke Godwin out of prison... I'm trying to quit being the Hero. After all that, you're still going to forgive me?"

"Of course."

"Can I be selfish? Is it really all right for me to do what I want to do instead of what the world or my blessing demands?"

Enjoying a slow life removed from the demands of the world was a luxury the Hero could never rightly be allowed. However, I would not cast aside Ruti's right to choose.

"Live how you like. That's what I do."

Ruti slowly placed her hands on my cheeks. She stared into my eyes for a long moment and then pressed her forehead to my chest.

"I'm so selfish, Big Brother. I'm a failure as the Hero." I couldn't see Ruti's face, but I could feel the warmth from her hands on my cheeks. "Please... Please don't hate me."

I put my hands on top of hers. "You're my little sister, Ruti. I will always love you."

"Thank you. I love you, too," she responded softly.

The moment took me back to that storm that had hit our village when we were kids.

*   *   *

My name is Tisse. I'm Ruti the Hero's friend. Rit and I finally reached the entrance to the ruins after Red had gone ahead of us.

"...I don't like this..."

Just as we were about to enter, an intense look crossed Rit's face.

"What is it?" I asked.

"I can sense someone on the mountain."

"You can?"

Rit had the Spirit Scout blessing, so her perception was better in more natural environments. However, this was also a place where adventurers came to gather medicinal herbs and where people from the nearby settlement came to log or hunt.

"Normal folk wouldn't venture this deep into the wilderness," Rit stated.

"You're saying this presence is close?"

I spun around. Two chimeras were lying where we had finished them off just a minute ago. If someone else was around, they would certainly have to be quite skilled.

"Probably. I can't say for sure, though," admitted Rit.

"I suppose it's whoever summoned that spirit drake," I replied.

"Yeah. What about footprints?"

Out in nature, Rit's Spirit Scout blessing allowed her to sense something as vague as another's whereabouts far off in the distance, but my Assassin blessing specialized in tracking skills. I was capable of recognizing characteristic footprints on stone pavement and picking people out of a crowd.

"There's evidence of three going into the ruins: Ms. Ruti, Godwin, and then Red. The only new prints since the last time I was here are Ms. Ruti's and Red's. Previously, there were two sets from about a month earlier—Red's and one other's."

"Someone else?" Rit inquired.

"Whoever it was appeared to have explored the upper level of the ruins once. They didn't return after that single pass."

As for Red's first trip, it seemed he'd only taken a quick look around to gather what he could. The interior of the ruins was the correct dampness for mushrooms and moss to grow in abundance. Mister Crawly Wawly seemed to enjoy the humidity, too, because his jewellike black eyes were glimmering as he peeked out of my bag.

"So another adventurer in Zoltan was investigating this place," deduced Rit. As we made our way into the ruins, she seemed to be pondering who that unknown other could have been.

*   *   *

When we reached Godwin's room, he shrank back in fear at the sight of Rit.

"Don't worry. I don't hold a grudge against you, and I'm not here to get revenge or anything," she assured.

"S-sorry 'bout that."

Rit smirked a little bit at seeing Godwin tremble. She made a point of drawing her sword to relish his reaction. She could be a bit childish at times.

"Where is Ms. Ruhr?"

When in Godwin's presence, I went by the alias Tifa, and Ms. Ruti went by Ruhr. My real name was not particularly problematic, but the moniker Ruti the Hero was known to just about everyone.

"She went off somewhere with that apothecary," Godwin hastily explained.

"Is that so?"

If so, then following Red's footsteps was the fastest way to find the two. Fortunately, their tracks were still fresh. Though without a high-level Tracking skill, it would be impossible to judge any tracks left on the strange material ancient elves made their floors from.

Rit turned around as we started to leave the room.

"What is it?" I asked.

She opened the item box at her waist and, after reciting the command word, pulled out a magic knife that emanated darkness, a chain mail tunic interwoven with sound-dampening fabric, a thunderstone that unleashed a flash of light when used, and a smoke wand that released a cloud of thick vapor when broken. She set them all on the floor.

"Rit?!" I exclaimed.

"I don't have any particular attachment to your life, Godwin, but apparently, you're a bit of a crucial person. There is a possibility that someone is going to break into these ruins. Someone who is at least as strong as I am. Maybe even more so. I doubt you can win against whoever it is, so use these to protect yourself if you need to."

"A-against someone better than you?! Are you kidding?! Take me with you!"

"We've got our hands full with another matter. If it looks like we can come back for you, we will." Then she took out a potion bottle—one that contained the spell Invisibility. "I'm leaving this here for you, too, but don't get your hopes up. This almost certainly won't work on whoever is nearby."

Godwin was muttering complaints as he picked up the items she had placed on the floor. "I'm beggin' ya here, don't go dragging me into a fight between a bunch of damn heroes."

"It's better than getting executed at least, right?" Rit said with a shrug.

Godwin slumped in surrender at that, sitting on the floor. Seeing him like that was so pitiful I felt just a little bit of sympathy for him. Mister Crawly Wawly raised his right leg, too, urging the Alchemist to cheer up.

∗   ∗   ∗

Had Ares not gone off to the airship, he would have discovered Red and been able to follow after him. Instead, he had been forced to rely on his magic to search around the mountain.

"It should be around here." He was scratching at his arm in frustration, muttering to himself.

Ares's spell used Albert's blood like a compass that pointed toward Ruti. When poured on the disk he was holding, the red liquid would react to the magic of Albert's contract and be pulled in Ruti's direction. Unfortunately, the container was a flat surface, not a sphere. It could not point up or down.

Ruti was in the archaic compound that spread out deep beneath the mountain.

"Why?! Why can't I find her?!" Ares cried, paying no heed to the blood flowing from his arm.

Shisandan was pondering what to do as he watched the Sage's reaction. His impression of Danan, the man whose form the Asura demon was borrowing, was that he was not a particularly bright man. Shisandan had not been able to steal Danan's memories, but when he had infiltrated Loggervia in the guise of Gaius, he had spoken with Danan several times. Ares hadn't discovered him yet, so he had to be doing a convincing enough job of playing the part.

Shisandan suspected that Ruti had already entered the ancient elf ruins. The reason they could not find her was because she was underground. However, that wasn't something an idiot like Danan would suggest.

Ares was a man with his back to the wall. It would even be fair to say he was unable to think clearly at present. At a fundamental level, Asura demons had entirely different values and philosophies from humans, elves, and even other demons. Shisandan had eaten many humans before and observed their memories, but even still, he could not comprehend humans' thought processes.

When he hid himself among them, he would plumb the memories of whoever he was imitating, choose situations that seemed the most similar, and act based on those recollections. Unfortunately, he had not gained any memories from Danan this time. As such, he hadn't spoken more than absolutely necessary, choosing to merely follow after Ares.

But at this rate, we won't get anywhere.

Among the memories Shisandan had consumed, there was one from a man who had been desperate, like Ares was now. Shisandan decided he would use that as his model.

"Hey, I just remembered, but apparently, there were ancient elf ruins on this mountain."

"And what of it?! Please spare me your prattle and just search for Ruti!" snapped Ares.

"No, I mean from what I heard, those ruins are underground."

"…Why didn't you say so sooner?!"

"Sorry, it totally slipped my mind."

"Kh, this is why I can't stand incompetents. Where is the site you speak of?!"

Did that go okay? I think I managed to fool him by acting like I thought that important tidbit was too trivial to bring up sooner.

Sensing no suspicion from Ares, Shisandan indulged in a bit of silent self-praise. It had been worth the wait to stand around first before bringing it up.

This one seems useful. I may not even need to deceive him for much longer. I might be able to draw him to my side.

If Shisandan revealed himself then and there, there was no chance he would be able to convince Ares to ally with him. After a rejection from the Hero and having his dream crushed, however? When all were to seem lost to Ares, and he discovered a way he might still achieve his aspirations, he'd surely take it. At that point, it wouldn't matter that it involved dirtying his hands a bit, right?

It's just a question of timing. As I am right now, I probably have no chance of winning against him.

For all Ares's faults, his magical power was the real deal. If at all possible, Shisandan would prefer to put things into motion after acquiring the artifacts that lay sleeping somewhere in the ancient elf ruins.

Shisandan was walking out in front as he plotted how to approach the task. Pondering how best to trap his target was one of his favorite pastimes. In that regard, the time he had tricked Rit in Loggervia had been extraordinarily gratifying.

While careful not to let Ares see, Shisandan cracked a sinister grin as he silently laid out his moves.

*   *   *

At about the same time, Danan was still sprinting along the path, his face red from the exertion. While he was far swifter than the average person due to his skills, he was still only halfway to the mountain.

"Dammit! At this rate, it'll all be over by the time I catch up!" he shouted as his legs pounded against the ground.

The merchants and other travelers he passed on the road ran screaming in the other direction, thinking he was a highway robber.

"Nrrrrrrrggggggh!!!" Danan psyched himself up, but no matter how much he tried, there was no dramatic increase in his speed. Just when he was starting to regret not having gotten a mount, he felt an oppressive presence above.

"What?! Another spirit drake?!"

It was a giant one, catching the wind in its wings as it flew through the air above him. It looked different from the first drake.

"Huh, that looks like Theodora's summons."

Every part of the creature's body, save its red wings, was covered in armor. Danan recalled that the spirit beasts Theodora summoned with her clerical arts had all sported the same sort of protective covering.

The Martial Artist knew next to nothing about magic, so he didn't comprehend that the difference between this creature and the one he'd seen earlier was that this one had been conjured from clerical arts, while Ares's mystical arts had summoned the other.

Theodora's powers borrowed strength from the domain of Victy, guardian of martyrs, one of Almighty Demis's three disciples. This limited Theodora in a way. She was only able to call upon spirit beasts whose attributes existed within Victy's domain. Those creatures she did summon manifested under the influence of Victy.

Ares could use clerical arts as well, but they relied on borrowing power from Larael, the guardian of hope, another of the three disciples. Invocations made through Larael had the same restriction on attributes, so Ares generally used mystical arts to avoid those restrictions.

The clerical arts largely drew power from one of the three

disciples, but those inclined toward evil could source it from San-nou, a legendary demon overlord said to have rebelled against Demis.

The spirit drake circled slowly over Danan's head. After seemingly spotting him, it immediately began a descent.

"Huh?"

Danan started clenching his fist and stopped running, getting excited as he wondered whether it might attack or not. While he understood that it was a bad habit of his to forget everything going on around him whenever he sensed a strong enemy, that was just how he was.

Ares had snidely chided him for it many times. It had caused problems once or twice when Danan had first joined up with the Hero. Very soon after, however, it miraculously seemed to stop creating trouble. Thinking back on it now, Danan understood that it had been because Gideon had a full grasp on all his party members' quirks and had worked to design the best deployments so that they could all fight at their best.

Things might have been different if he had just explained as much. No point thinking about that now, I guess. I've got a spirit drake right in front of me to deal with first.

When the drake was low enough that it's head was clearly visible, it spread its wings wide and slowed its glide.

"Danan! It's me!" an armored woman shouted as she leaned out from the drake's back.

"Theodora?!"

As far as Danan knew, she should have been far away.

$$*\qquad\qquad*\qquad\qquad*$$

"This sure is convenient."

This was the second time in Danan's life that he had ridden on a spirit drake. The first had been when they had traveled to Gandor of the Wind's hideout. They had been working together with the lightning dragons to break through Gandor's wyvern knights, but Ares had insisted he fly a spirit drake so he could do as he pleased, and Danan had gone along to keep him safe.

Back then, there hadn't been any time to comment about how nice riding was between all his complaints whenever Ares's questionable steering got them into a dangerous situation.

"Why didn't you use one of these fellas more often?" Danan asked Theodora, who was sitting in front of him with the drake's reins in her hands.

"It stands out too much. There aren't that many mages capable of summoning a spirit drake, and if the demon lord's forces saw one, they would surely be on their guard."

"Makes sense," Danan accepted. Spotting such an unusual beast from the ground wasn't too difficult. Gideon had run off precisely because he'd seen that spirit drake earlier.

"So who's he?" With a finger, Danan indicated the man sitting behind him.

"My name is Albert, sir. It's an honor to meet you. I've heard tales of your victories against the demon lord's army, even way out in Zoltan. It's a rather long story, but I'm an adventurer who is currently accompanying Theodora." Albert introduced himself with a respectful bow.

Danan nodded before quickly losing interest. "Anyway, that was great timing. Now I can get to the mountain in no time."

"Are you seriously not going to ask why I'm here? The timing doesn't seem odd to you at all?" inquired Theodora.

"Not like I'd figure anything out even if I did think about things like that. The Hero's somewhere on the mountain, and she needs us. That's enough for me."

"...You really are a simple man," Theodora replied with a wry smile.

There was a trace of envy in her expression, but Danan was not the sort who'd notice that.

"I picked you up because I want you to be there for it, whatever result might come of the choices we make," stated Theodora.

"?"

"It's fine if you don't get what I mean. Do as you please. I'll act how I see fit, too."

"Roger. I'm not sure I get it, but isn't that obvious? We'll both do what we want. That's how it should be," Danan responded with a hearty laugh.

Albert was dumbfounded. This was another entirely different sort of hero from Ares or Theodora.

*   *   *

Once Ruti had calmed down, we headed back out into the corridor.

"Red!"

No sooner had we stepped out than we saw Rit and Tisse running toward us.

"That was fast," I remarked.

"We were in a bit of a hurry," Rit said with a smile.

Ruti looked expressionless, but her cheeks were turning ever so slightly redder. It was what she did when she was feeling happy.

"Thank you," Ruti murmured.

The four of us returned to Godwin's room to get what information we could about Devil's Blessing.

From what the contract demon had said, the principle behind the substance was that it used its core ingredient, an ax demon's heart, to create a demon blessing that suppressed the user's natural one. However...

"That was how the contract demon explained it to me, too," Ruti added, before tilting her head. "But the Hero's blessing treats the effects of a demon's heart as a curse, eliminating it. So when I drank it, I did not develop an ax demon blessing."

"Then how is your innate blessing being suppressed?" I inquired.

Ruti tilted her head. "The blessing I developed is one without a name."

"Nameless?" I repeated, at a loss.

"Yes. When I connect with it, there aren't any skills or impulses. It's just there."

What could that be? I'd done lots of research on blessings, so I felt confident that I knew more than most on the subject, but I'd never heard of this before. Was it really a blessing?

"My levels are definitely shifting to that nameless blessing, and the Hero's urges are weakening."

"If there aren't any impulses, and if that blessing's level gets higher than your natural one's, does that mean there won't be any murderous fits?" Rit asked, hopefulness apparent in her voice.

Ax demon blessings had caused the brutal attacks that had plagued Zoltan a while back. If this nameless thing in Ruti really didn't have any compulsions, then there was no danger.

"A blessing with no name… On top of being a complete unknown, it's like no other blessing in existence. Not knowing what it might be capable of is ominous in its own way," I said.

Every blessing had a role. Regardless of how powerful or weak a Divine Blessing was, its name, urges, and skills were a means for the bearer to interpret their assigned lot in life and gain the abilities necessary to fulfill that role.

So then, what could one divine from a blessing with no identifiable qualities?

"There's a lot that's still in the dark. I'd like to ask Godwin, since he's an actual Alchemist," I stated.

We continued to discuss it as we made our way back to Godwin's room. As Ruti had blown the door off the wall, we could see the man before entering. He twitched when he heard our approach.

"D-don't scare me like that." Godwin breathed a sigh of relief after realizing we weren't the enemy Rit had warned him of earlier.

"I know this is sudden, but I want to know everything you know about Devil's Blessing," I said.

Unraveling all this was doubtlessly going to be difficult, but we had to face the mystery of this demonic medicine head-on.

*   *   *

"Basically, Devil's Blessing was created as a kind of stopper meant to limit the effects of its base—the substance that creates that nameless blessing. It achieves this by causing a demon blessing to develop instead of the nameless one and by transferring levels to it. With the unaltered, original drug, your innate blessing's level won't go down. Even if you didn't have an immunity to curses, Devil's Blessing was unnecessary."

This was the hypothesis that Godwin presented to us when pressed for details about Devil's Blessing. He had used one of his skills to analyze the medicine.

"So is the part about limiting urges something added later, too? Or was it part of the original compound?" I questioned.

"Hard to say. There's a possibility the nameless blessing might limit the impulses of your natural one without decreasing its level. Still, the drug's original purpose was to create that nameless blessing."

"So then the part about it weakening your innate blessing to increase the efficiency of leveling that the demon told Ruhr about was not its original usage?" I queried.

"Yeah, and that bit about the levels in the new blessing returning after a week wasn't an original part of how the substance worked, either."

Things were just getting more and more baffling. The demons' alterations seemed designed to destroy the original drug's effects.

"What about the dependency and narcotic effects?" Ruti asked.

She was the one actually taking the medicine, so that was a critical point. While she could nullify adverse effects with her immunities, if her blessing level kept shifting, it was possible that she could lose such impunity.

"That's just a problem with the ingredients. It uses dwarven blackfire peppers, which are quite addictive. They are banned here in Zoltan, so acquiring them actually proved to be the most challenging part of the whole process. There's still a lot of them left in Bighawk's hidden stockroom for now, though."

"Is there any substitute for them?" I inquired.

"I'm just a washed-up Alchemist who wound up with the Thieves Guild. Don't go askin' me to figure out any modifications to the recipe."

Godwin had been a key member of the Thieves Guild under Bighawk, but he was by no means exceptionally knowledgeable when it came to alchemy.

I glanced down at the notes the man had written from his analysis and considered the problem. Still, there just wasn't enough there for me to make a definitive statement one way or the other about replacements for the dwarven blackfire peppers.

With Ruti's Healing Hands, she could completely cure any addiction or overdose. And there were high-level healers in most large cities capable of magics that could heal the medicine's damage. Such services demanded payment, of course, but such prices were little more than pocket change to someone of Ruti's means.

I suppose we can ignore the dwarven blackfire peppers for now... though I'd like to remove them from the equation at some point.

"The murderous impulses started occurring when the demon's blessing surpassed the innate blessing in level. What do you think will happen when this nameless blessing surpasses Ruhr's innate blessing?" I asked.

"I can't say for sure, but those violent urges came from the ax demon's blessing. If a blessing that doesn't have any impulses surpasses her innate one, then I'd assume nothing in particular would happen," concluded Godwin.

He's got the same assumption I have, I thought.

"So in sum, what are we looking at?" Tisse asked.

"Hmm. For the time being, it looks like the risk is minimal. We have to be careful about Ruhr's level getting too low. Still, I don't think we'll have to worry about her getting violent."

Ruti's eyes widened a bit at that. She had probably been fretting over whether we would tell her not to take the substance anymore.

"From what I can tell, demons added all the dangerous parts after the fact. I want to investigate the recipe in more detail myself, but for the moment, I think it is okay to use it to suppress urges until we find another way," I decided.

Never would I have guessed that my knowledge of medicine would wind up being such a boon for Ruti. I felt a small surge of pride when I saw that she seemed happy.

"As for other issues, there's the problem of Zoltan being viewed as problematic after the incident with Devil's Blessing. Forget dwarven blackfire peppers, just trying to get our hands on the other special ingredients will draw the attention of Zoltan's authorities."

"What about just growing the things we need here on the mountain?" Rit proposed.

"That's easy enough in theory, but it's pretty difficult to raise plants brought in from another climate. Though there's no reason not to try, either," I replied.

"Oh."

"And I'll look into the possibility of substituting some of the ingredients. It's possible that the demons intentionally used certain additives to produce a more addictive medicine."

Ruti had made it clear that the contract demon had been devout in its faith in Demis. While that seemed contrary to expectation, it made sense that demons who strictly adhered to what their blessings wanted would be faithful believers of Demis, too. Yet those loyalists had preserved the method of producing a medicine that created a new blessing, something that was unquestionably an act of rebellion against God.

The reason they had done so was likely because, in the form of Devil's Blessing, the drug was a way to develop one's innate blessing even further. Still, the demons recognized that this incredible medicine could also be used to resist Demis's designs.

Perhaps that was why the altered recipe called for such rare and addictive ingredients—to prevent any unintended spread. Overdoses and addiction were a lethal problem for the average person.

"It's still difficult to reconcile demons being such ardent believers...," I muttered to myself.

When I found some time with Ruti, I wanted to discuss that point in more detail. Back then, in the Hero's party, Ruti and I had spent many sleepless nights debating all sorts of things about the nature of the world. I looked forward to doing that again when we were back home in Zoltan.

That would be nice.

"What is it, Big Brother?" Noticing my gaze, Ruti tilted her head. I just smiled to let her know it was nothing problematic. "Okay," she responded with a nod. It looked like her cheeks had reddened slightly.

"Something's coming," Tisse suddenly whispered so that only those in the room would hear.

Save for Godwin, we all quickly drew our weapons and focused. Godwin scurried behind us when I gave the signal.

"I-I'm sure it will be fine with you guys here...," he muttered nervously.

Ruti was not paying any attention to him as she slowly approached the doorway out to the corridor.

Using the Enhanced Detection skill that the Hero blessing provided, every one of Ruti's senses became as perceptive as her vision, allowing her to discern the slightest vibrations, changes in heat, smells, and such. Tisse's Assassin ability to sense presences covered a wider range, but Ruti's skill was superior in close quarters since it allowed her to see through walls.

"It's an iron snake," Ruti whispered.

A small object flew out from the shadows at the entrance. But the moment it appeared, Ruti's sword was already bearing down on it, splitting the iron snake before it had any chance to test its fangs.

"An iron snake? What's one of those doing here?" Rit's face was clouded.

Iron snakes were a type of golem created from a combination of magic and alchemy. The serpent-shaped metal constructs were about thirty centimeters long. While they weren't very powerful, they were stealthy and able to slip into all sorts of openings, making the things quite versatile. On top of that, they had a mapping capability and the power to display what they observed to their controller. Iron snakes were perfectly suited to matters of espionage.

"It's an entirely different kind of golem from the clockwork ones typically found in places like this. There's no record of iron snakes in ancient elf ruins anywhere else," I said.

"Someone else must be here. They're concealing themself with magic, but I can just barely detect a faint presence when I focus on it," Tisse stated. Mister Crawly Wawly popped his head out of her bag to try to convey something to her. "According to Mister Crawly Wawly, two humans have trod on the threads he laid out." Her spider nodded, confirming what she said.

In the time he had been together with Tisse, Mister Crawly Wawly had raised his level, and apparently, he could discern the general size and shape of creatures who touched his silk from the vibrations transmitted through it.

"Two people, huh?" I whispered.

The one who'd summoned the spirit drake and some ally, maybe? It was hard to say whether they had spotted us below on the mountain path. Regardless, they were aware of the iron snake's destruction.

"...Is it Shisandan?" Rit wondered quietly. Her expression was filled with a mix of unease and a dark anticipation.

*   *   *

"Hey, wouldn't it be better if Ms. Ruhr was the one protecting me?" Godwin whined pitifully.

"You're stuck with me, so just suck it up."

Ruti and Rit stood at the head of the group with Tisse behind them, Godwin behind her, and I brought up the rear to protect the Alchemist if we were assailed from behind.

"But you're the least reliable one of them."

"Ever tactful, I see."

"This is a life-or-death situation!"

Godwin was a high-level Alchemist—by Zoltan standard anyway. However, he couldn't hold a candle to the class of opponents the Hero regularly engaged with, and he understood that as well as anyone else here. That was why we had taken this formation.

Ruti twitched in reaction to something behind us. I immediately drew one of the throwing knives I had borrowed from Rit and let it fly. The weapon caught another iron snake that had been sneaking toward us and destroyed it.

My sister and I did not need words to communicate. I was confident in my ability to act how she intended from a single glance alone. Countless battles together had forged our sibling bond into a kind of second-nature response.

It wouldn't be hyperbole to say that the moment she noticed something with her extremely heightened perception, it was also shared with me.

"I know they aren't exactly built to last, but still, one-shotting an iron golem with a throwing knife? Why the hell are you an apothecary? Did you screw something up and have to go into hiding or

something?" Godwin quietly asked in awe when he saw the little
golem's shattered head.

✳   ✳   ✳

Tisse used a skill, standing still and focusing as she searched for
any more unwelcome guests. "The iron snakes have left this level,"
she declared after a moment.

We had come across a total of four iron snakes and destroyed all
of them. However, Tisse had sensed at least seven of the little things
earlier. That meant at least three of them had been pulled away from
this floor.

"What about the people?" I questioned.

"They're still using a spell to hide, so I can't pin down their loca-
tions, but I think one of them has moved below the surface," the
Assassin replied.

"Splitting up?" Rit seemed surprised. If this pair was hostile, them
parting was a decision in our favor. "They must know we broke the
iron snakes, right? Even if we assume these two are entirely unre-
lated to Shisandan or Devil's Blessing stuff, they must recognize by
now that there is a threat down here. So why split up?"

"It's certainly odd. They may be using magic or a martial art that
can throw off my perception, but…" Tisse trailed off.

The girl was one of the best Assassins around. Only a few could
hope to disguise themselves from her senses. Was there anyone
truly capable of disrupting her perception so thoroughly?

"Stay on guard. Be ready to react in case they somehow did manage to trick Tisse's reading, but for now, let's assume she's correct,"
I stated.

"Understood." Ruti nodded at my proposal. No sooner had she
done so than her mouth curved ever so slightly into a smile.

"Something up?" I inquired.

"The situation is what it is, but…I'm happy. It's been so long since you've fired off directions like that…" Ruti was looking me straight in the eyes as she said that, but she quickly reverted to a serious expression and faced forward again.

*   *   *

Everyone, even Godwin, noticed the change.

"Something's coming!" Rit called out sharply.

"Mister Crawly Wawly's webs have all been torn apart! It's a swarm of things no bigger than fingernails!"

"Ruti! Rit! Use Levitate!"

Ruti and Rit, the two who could use the spell, quickly cast it on everyone. Suddenly, we were all hovering slightly above the ground, waiting for the horde that had suddenly appeared.

"Is it spiders? Ants? It can't be parasitic grubs, right?" Godwin listed the sorts of swarms adventurers often encountered. Disregarding such threats simply because they were insects or arachnids was foolhardy. You couldn't defeat a horde of bugs with conventional weapons. Magic or fire were typically the best options. They could be truly dangerous, easily capable of taking down the unprepared. However, the little things that came skittering into sight weren't ants or spiders.

"Eeeep!" Godwin screamed reflexively at the sight of them filling the floor. Rit gasped and shuddered, too.

"Plague Eyes…," I muttered.

They were crying human eyes. Red, tentacle-like blood vessels extended from the backs of the things, and they used those to crawl along the floor. That alone would have been repulsive, but after moving around for a bit, the eyeballs would start to bubble and split apart. The frothing liquid from inside spawned more of their kind.

"It's a high-level mystic art, a combination of summoning magic and necromancy that uses the eyes of dead humans who bore intense grudges as a medium. The conjured things continue to create more of themselves," I explained. The crying eyes filling the floor looked up at us, floating in the air. It was a scene that made even my hair stand on end. "They can't be controlled and will keep increasing until the magic that first made them runs out. It's meant to overrun anyone on the ground. That said, they're still the result of a summoning spell, so whoever cast it will be aware if any eyes are killed. I've heard stories about some using that method to locate an enemy."

"Attacking them will alert their master to us?" Tisse asked.

"Pretty much. Plague Eyes cover a wide area. No one would bother using them if they knew where their quarry was already. It's fortunate that Levitate allows us to evade them," I replied.

Conjuring such disgusting things was no small feat, but the method was not without its weaknesses. All we needed to do was keep floating in the air until its effect ran out.

"...Weren't they trying to locate us using those iron snakes?" Rit asked.

"Perhaps the two of them are unable to share information for some reason?" proposed Tisse.

There was no denying that using Plague Eyes here was odd. But while I was grappling with the implications of that decision, Ruti just furrowed her brow impatiently.

"We're not going to figure it out by guessing. We should just ask directly."

"Huh?" I managed before Ruti signed something arcane with her left hand.

"Judgment Lightning."

"Wha—?!"

An intense bolt struck the eyeball-flooded floor and raced through the corridor.

The spells afforded by the Divine Blessing of the Hero were cost inefficient but rivaled Archmage and Sage blessings in terms of immediate output. They wielded a power that made a mockery of all the magic swordsman-type blessings that struggled to balance bladework with spells.

Ruti's temple twitched. "Someone blocked it," she muttered, dropping to the ground with her sword drawn. She started running.

"Wait! Don't go off alone! Rit, Tisse! Keep Godwin safe, but try to catch up as soon as you can!" I took off after Ruti without waiting for them to respond.

She hadn't ever gone off on her own like this while I had been in the party.

Is this how she's been fighting since I left?

"Ruti!" I called.

"Around that corner."

Though I'd caught up to her, I didn't even have time to get a warning out before she turned at an intersection. Naturally, I followed after, but seeing the figure standing there made me forget myself for a moment.

"Ruti! I finally found you!"

"Ares?!"

Standing there was Ares the Sage, the man who had driven me from my sister's side. In his present state, he looked nothing like the man I had once known.

Ares's handsome features had made him popular with women back in Central, but now his hair was a wild mess, and his cheeks were sunken. Formerly calm and discerning eyes were now wide and bloodshot, resembling the dead little things fading away in bubbling foam on the floor.

"Let's go defeat the demon lord, Ruti. The Hero is the only one who can save the world. And I must be there at your side. The Hero and the Sage. We've nothing to fear from any demon lord with such Divine Blessings at our disposal."

"A-Ares, what happened to you...?" I asked.

Keeping up appearances had been paramount to him. Even when we were on the road, he'd always taken care to maintain himself. It made how he looked now all the more shocking.

"Come, Ruti. Take my hand. You realized we don't need anyone else, right? That's why you left? I agree. Danan, Theodora, Yarandrala, Tisse, Gideon… They were all just getting in our way. Useless scoundrels who could do nothing more than complain. But we can defeat the demon lord together, just the two of us. A glorious future awaits."

Ares did not respond to my words. His cheeks were twitching in a spastic smile as he extended his hand to Ruti.

"Ares." Ruti's voice was soft, and she was gazing at him almost piteously.

"Ruti…"

"I'm not going to travel with you anymore."

"Huh?"

"I don't know what comes next, but my journey with you has reached its end. My time as the Hero is over. Now I'm only Ruti."

What Ares needed, what he required, wasn't Ruti. It was the Hero. That was why Ruti closed the book on her quest with Ares. It was a parting, but in her own way, my little sister was also drawing a line of sorts with a man she had known for very long.

Ares looked down, smile still pasted across his face. "You're too kind. You feel a need to help a hopeless cause like Gideon. That's why you're choosing a man with a worthless blessing over me. Because you can't bear to cast aside that hindrance, right?"

"You've got it wrong, Ares, Ruti is—"

"Silence!"

Ares moved his hand in a practiced motion.

"Ares?! What are yo—? Gh!!!" The next thing I knew, his Force Shot spell had sent me flying. I slammed into the wall behind me with a loud crash. The impact knocked the air from my lungs, and I couldn't breathe for a moment. Unable to hold on, I dropped to one knee.

"There! Now it's all fine, Ruti! Let us be off to vanquish the demon lord!" Ares faced Ruti with arms wide open, almost like he was sure that she would jump into his embrace. Ruti did leap forward, but not in the way Ares had hoped.

"Even now, you still don't see *me*."

"Huh?" Shocked, Ares looked down and discovered Ruti's sword sticking out of his stomach. "Agh! Ahhhhhhhhhhhhhhhhhhhh?!"

Disbelief was plain on Ares's face. His wide eyes looked down to gaze at the blood flowing from his gut. Ruti retracted her blade without any hesitation.

"I'm not kind at all."

"Ugwahhhhhhhhhh! Wh-why? This is a misunderstanding! I'm Ares the Sage! Why did you stab me...?"

"I avoided piercing anything vital. Healing yourself with magic shouldn't be too much trouble. This is my answer. I don't feel conflicted about running you through for hurting someone important to me. If Big Brother had been seriously wounded, I would have killed you," Ruti stated matter-of-factly. Then she turned her back on him and walked over to me. "Are you okay, Big Brother? Wait just a second, and I'll heal you."

"Ah, yeah, please."

Thankfully, my injury wasn't anything grievous. Force Shot was a spell better suited to knocking targets away than destroying them. With my high blessing level, it amounted to a few bruises and scrapes.

"R-Ruti...my wound is more serious... Healing...please...," Ares pleaded as he clutched at his stomach. Yet Ruti did not even turn back to look at him.

"I'm not the Hero. And I'm never going to help you again."

She left no room at all for misinterpretation, rejecting Ares altogether.

Chapter 3

- - - - - - - - -

Diverging Paths

My name is Ares Srowa. By all rights, I should have been Ares *of* Srowa, but my family was stripped of its territory. Thus, I was not Ares of the land of Srowa but merely Ares Srowa. I was the second son of Marquis Srowa. I have two older sisters.

There was a time when I had a brother, the eldest son, but he became a page in the Bahamut Knights to raise his status, and while carrying lances for an elderly warrior, he was struck by a bandit's stray arrow and died pointlessly.

My brother was born with the Divine Blessing of the Cavalier, but he met his end before even earning a steed. All he did was carry spare lances for those knights who broke theirs. He never had a chance to make use of his Cavalier skills.

My two sisters left our family some time ago—sold off in political marriages. Each was wed to a wealthy merchant's son to lend an aristocratic dignity to plebeians with nothing but money to their names.

"It's a blessing that you were born. Ares the Sage will be the hope of our family."

Growing up, my father said those words to me countless times. They became a mantra to him.

The Divine Blessing of the Sage. It was an incredibly rare blessing that could use both the mystic arts of mage-style blessings and the clerical arts of cleric-line blessings. In matters of magic, it is unmatched.

My father's blessing was Fighter, a blessing that you could find on any corner in any town. Never had I thought him fit to be head of a noble household. He was quite aware of this inadequacy, too. It was clear from his demeanor that he struggled with his position. That much was to be expected, I suppose. For what proper marquis would lower his head to a peasant contractor to seek work as an adventurer to earn money?

To make up for his own failure, my father wished for my brother and me to become the dignified aristocrats he never could. The world I was raised in was a hopelessly foolish place.

Sage blessing possessed a unique skill, one that could only be accessed by those with either the Sage blessing or the Saint blessing. It allowed the user to appraise another's blessing.

Though it required significant mental focus, the results spoke for themselves. I could see others' blessings and levels—their true natures.

The mere ability to use Appraisal was enough to guarantee someone with a Sage blessing a warm welcome in any country. That was why my father, the disgraced marquis, had placed all his hopes on me.

Alas, he misunderstood. I held my family in contempt. It was true that with Appraisal alone, I would be guaranteed a certain level of stature. If I worked thirty years, I could reclaim a land title befitting a minor earl or viscount. However, no amount of study or work could achieve anything befitting a marquis.

I despised my homeland. Throughout my life, I used Appraisal on all sorts of people of varying social standing, peeking into their blessings as I pleased. In doing that, I realized that there were but two types in this country. Those who were energetic and confident in everything they did, and those who dawdled, always made mistakes, and only ever opened their mouths to complain.

As a Sage, I quickly understood the reason for that. Some had

jobs that aligned well with their blessings, and some did not. This
wasn't a profound revelation. I had figured that much out long ago,
having observed my father.

I understood what it meant to attain happiness. Everyone should
live as ordained by God. That was the path to a fulfilling life. Since
that was the case, how should I, a Sage, live my life?

The moment I first laid eyes on the Hero, I knew what my calling
was. As the wisest man, I would guide the Hero, fight alongside her,
and then, having destroyed the demon lord, I would set this irratio-
nal world right. All would live in accordance with their blessings. I
would manage the world as the embodiment of Almighty Demis's
holy will.

The reason I was born was not to restore the honor of my house—a
trivial matter before the scale of the world. No, my father's dream,
that of my brother who died before I ever knew him, both of those
were minor irrelevances that held no meaning at all to me.

I was born to rule over this world and become its magnificent
emperor.

✳   ✳   ✳

"I'm a Sage. This is... I haven't achieved anything yet...no territory, no revolution, no holy war...," Ares muttered as he blankly
stared at his blood pooling around his feet. Perhaps tasting a failure
that a Sage should never know had distracted him from healing his
wound.

"Why? Why can't the Hero live as she should? The Guide blessing
is worthless garbage that should have just stayed behind in the capital... Why have I, a Sage, been forsaken? Left bleeding out here...
Fools, the lot of them, fools. People are so foolish. Dammit...
dammit..."

Ares doubled over and grabbed his stomach, blood dripping from
his mouth as he clenched his teeth and continued to curse all but

himself. Even though he knew it was meaningless, he could not stop the hatred overflowing from within.

From the day he had pushed Gideon out of the party, nothing had gone as he'd planned. That fact demanded he acknowledge the worthless blessing Guide as superior to Sage. Ares had disproven his own tenet that one must live in a manner befitting their blessing.

The pillar supporting his spirit had crumbled. In his current state, he was incapable of noticing the shadow drawing near.

"Are you okay?"

Hearing a voice, Ares turned his bloodless, ghostlike visage toward the sound. What greeted him was a young man with dark skin. There was a long, slightly curved sword hanging at his waist, and he wore a cloak with iron scraps woven into it.

"Who are you...?" Ares weakly demanded.

"I'm Bui, an adventurer, as you can see. More to the point, though, that wound looks pretty bad. Do you need help?"

Bui held out an Extra Cure potion. Ares stared for a moment before a spark of life returned to his eyes, and he cast Extra Cure on himself.

"Oh, you can use Healer magic. My apologies for the assumption," remarked Bui, a cheap smile on his face. Ares narrowed his eyes.

"I see you, Asura demon." The man had used Appraisal and seen that Bui did not have a blessing. He would have noticed the same if he'd done as much when Shisandan was disguised as Danan, of course, but the skill required focus. Ares was not the type to waste effort on someone he knew unless given reason to doubt them.

This was a different situation. Ares was not so naive as to trust an adventurer who'd conveniently appeared out of nowhere in an ancient ruin.

Seeing that, Bui, or rather Shisandan, curled his lips into a pleased smirk. "That's the Sage for you. Saw through me, huh?" the demon remarked, subtly appealing to Ares's pride.

Still, Ares remained on guard, ready to hurl the spell he had queued up at any moment. However, fighting solo as a magic user was not an optimal scenario.

Summoning some help is the first order of business.

Having a spirit beast for protection was the classic move, but Ares was already within the Asura demon's range. He could feel a chill run down his spine.

This is all because of Gideon!

His blood ran cold, but a scorching hatred consumed his mind. Ares was determined to unleash all that anger as destructive magic, even if it meant dying here. Curiously, almost as though capable of peering into Ares's heart, Shisandan stepped back.

"I have no intention of fighting you, Sage."

"What *is* your aim then?"

"I saw how the Hero cast you aside."

"WATCH YOUR TONGUE!!!"

Infuriated, Ares activated his summoning spell. A spirit dire tiger leaped out at Shisandan with fangs bared, but the demon handily split the beast with a single slash.

"Calm yourself. I'm not here to rub salt in your wounds. What do you say? How about we form a temporary alliance?"

"Huh? Do you take me a fool? Why would I, a member of the Hero's party, join with a demon?"

"The Hero's party, huh?" Shisandan's false form grinned. In his rage, Ares could feel the thump of his heart filling his head. "Tell me, do you know why you were expunged from that little band?"

"Because of a fool named Gideon, who has bewitched the Hero," Ares replied immediately.

"That's right." Not expecting a demon to agree with him, Ares was taken aback by the response. "If blessings are the roles given by Demis, then the demon lord and the Hero fighting is not only destined but just and natural. We in the demon lord's army desire nothing more than for the Hero to rise up and battle the demon lord."

"...You mean to say that the demon lord is merely attempting to fulfill their ordained role?"

"Precisely. Because the balance of power between the two continents grows stale, the Hero and the demon lord must clash. The result of their conflict will upset the stagnant equilibrium. After a time, a new Hero and demon lord appear, and the cycle will continue. These wars have helped develop the world. Civilization, like blessings, can only advance through hardship. After all, the capabilities of the people and demons who lead are determined by the level of their blessings. A large-scale war weeds out the weak while the powerful gain levels. And the world advances to a new age on the backs of those chosen by Divine Blessings."

"Divine Blessings and civilization are the same… That…is something I have never considered before."

Ares was enraptured. Conversely, it was all Shisandan could do not to scowl in disgust at the absurd idea. The philosophy he outlined was that of the former demon lord. To Asura demons that possessed no blessings, the ideology was a wondrous farce and nothing more. By what logic did advancements in fields like farming or construction occur through combat? Asura demons saw the shackles of Divine Blessings as ludicrous.

Still, the debased concept served its purpose, earning Ares's trust. Shisandan judged that it was about time to get to the main point.

"A relic of the first Hero lays beneath the ground here in these ruins. So what do you say? We can continue our fight after retrieving it."

"A relic of the first Hero?!"

"If you give that to the current Hero, I'm sure it will make her remember her duty. She will realize that individuality is trivial to the Hero."

"Individuality? What do you mean? Wait…there is no way that a member of the demon lord's army like you would just hand over something so valuable," Ares said, dubious.

"As things stand, the Hero will abandon her role. If she does, the relic will be worthless anyway."

"That's…"

The outline of Shisandan's body warped, and he transformed into a six-armed demon.

"One as wise as you may even come to understand why the Hero exists and what you should do upon glimpsing the relic..." The demon's whispers seeped into Ares's mind. "Even for an Asura like myself, it will be difficult to proceed any further alone. I need your strength, Sage."

For Ares, who Ruti had cast aside, those words hit home. There was no way he could refuse.

*   *   *

Ruti and I headed back to the others. It did not take long to reunite, since they had been following behind us. When we mentioned we had run into Ares, Rit looked relieved, Tisse seemed shocked, and Godwin had no clue what was happening.

"Ares being here would explain the spirit drake," Ruti stated.

Tisse nodded in agreement.

He was undoubtedly the greatest mage in the world, but...

"Ares's presence concerns me, but I'm more worried about the other person who was supposed to be with him," I said.

It appeared that Ares had left his anonymous companion behind when he went underground. Anything that befell that person after the split-up was unclear. From what Tisse said, this other person was even more skilled at concealing themselves than Ares. Ruti and I should have asked Ares about that when we'd had the chance, but I guess that hadn't been much of an option.

"Maybe it was Theodora." Rit voiced the obvious theory.

"Normally, that might be the case, but if it's her, them splitting up doesn't make sense. Theodora would never do something so dangerous as venturing through ancient elf ruins on her own, not unless there was some special reason. She's someone who prioritizes logic over emotion," I replied.

"Now that you mention it, I did get that kind of feeling from her," Tisse appended.

Theodora wasn't the type to act alone in this sort of situation. I'd never been given reason to assume she possessed any knowledge about golems like iron snakes before, either.

Golems did not require any skill to control, but they did demand a high level of intelligence and precise manipulation of magic power. Theoretically, anyone with a blessing that could use magic could command them, but the number of people who could do so well was low.

The mechanical things weren't exactly cheap, either. Still, the main reason that golems, potentially mass-producible workers who never tired, didn't end up taking over all manual labor was that they were so difficult to control.

"In which case, did Ares find a new ally after Ruti left?" Rit asked.

"I guess so," I answered.

We returned to the room with Godwin's makeshift laboratory. I lit the fire and started making an herbal tea using a pot lying around. Ruti and I would both need a little bit of time to calm down. Everyone fell silent for a few minutes.

"Man, how long am I gonna have to be locked up in these ruins anyway? If it's just making medicine, there's no reason I can't do it in some other town, right?" Godwin muttered to himself as he sipped the steaming tea.

When Ruti turned toward him, however, he frantically corrected himself.

"I-it's not like it's even been a month here, so I'm not tryin' to complain or anything."

He really was totally terrified of her.

"I'll consider it." Ruti seemed remorseful for the situation she had put Godwin in. Not that he was aware of that. Misunderstanding entirely, the man was falling over himself to apologize.

Tisse and I just watched, almost feeling bad for him but not quite.

"So then…maybe Shisandan is involved?" Rit murmured.

"Shisandan, huh?" That had totally slipped my mind because of the shock of seeing Ares again.

"But Mr. Ares is a Sage. He would be able to recognize an Asura demon that did not have a blessing," protested Tisse.

"That's not guaranteed. Ares never uses Appraisal on a person he has met before. Back in Loggervia, he didn't notice when Shisandan took Gaius's form partway through our time there," I corrected.

"Right. And Shisandan can turn into Danan," added Rit.

It wouldn't be surprising at all to learn that Ares was unknowingly in cahoots with the demon.

"So then the iron snakes were Shisandan's? What for?" Tisse inquired.

My first thought was that Shisandan was searching for Ruti. It made sense that the demon lord's forces would be after the Hero. Yet even after discovering her via the iron snakes, he had chosen to leave us be and venture deeper into the ruins. And if he had intended to get the drop on us by appearing as Danan, it would have been better not to use the iron snakes and just search for us with Ares.

"If the constructs weren't for us, then they must have been scouring the complex," Ruti deduced.

"Yeah, Dreadonna's forces have been gathering weapons and treasures from ancient sites all across Avalon. It's possible that plundering has become just another one of their goals, and that might be why Shisandan is here," I posited.

However, Dreadonna's pillaging had only occurred in areas already under their control. While Zoltan did not have much in the way of defenses, there were no known cases of the demon lord's army venturing so from their supply lines. The risk for them seemed high. It still didn't add up.

"Wait a moment," Tisse interjected.

"What is it?"

"Mr. Ares is on the move. And it's faint, but I sense one other person with him."

"They've reunited?" Rit stood up. "Even if there's only a chance that it's Shisandan, I can't just stand by."

"Facing Ares again gives me pause, but if he's being tricked, he deserves to know," I said.

The Sage and I had our differences, but leaving him to an Asura demon was still wrong. Wasting no time, we set out in search of Ares.

Unfortunately, he was no longer on the same floor as us by that point.

✳   ✳   ✳

"Th-this is...?!" The sight before Ares struck him speechless. Such verdant green was entirely at odds with the cold, hard material that made up ancient elf ruins.

Whatever equipment had originally been in the room had crumbled long ago, and granite caskets lined the chamber. Inside were desiccated wood elf mummies, lying there holding swords that bore no trace of rust despite centuries of age.

"Wood elves believed in the importance of the cycle of nature. Their custom in death was to perform funeral rites and then leave the bodies in the forest to be eaten by animals and return from whence they came. I see... What lays beyond this point was something they wished so deeply to protect that they were willing to break from that sacred tradition," Shisandan, as Bui, said with a smirk. "The Hero's relic is near."

A vague unease swelled in Ares's chest.

Why had the wood elves hidden an artifact left by the first Hero? Such an object was undoubtedly a symbol of hope. What could be gained by stowing it away without so much as a story that whispered of its existence?

The two proceeded deeper, passing the mummified elves, who stared at them with empty eyes. Shisandan hummed to himself, though he sneered at the corpses.

It almost felt like the room was filled with a churning animosity. Ares shuddered, feeling a sudden chill. Despite his foreboding sense, the wood elves did not rise as undead. They were merely crumbling bodies. It was not as if any number of undead—beings without blessings—was a match for a Sage and an Asura demon anyway.

As Ares and Shisandan approached the exit on the chamber's far side, the pair suddenly detected an intense hostility. Shisandan reflexively drew his sword. The next moment, an elven blade lanced straight for him. Gripping his own weapon in both hands, he deflected the attack. It was a mighty blow that left Shisandan's fingers numb after the impact.

"Who's there?"

One of the wood elves rose with a sliding sound. And then it collapsed to the floor with a *thud*.

"D-Danan?!" Ares shouted.

The Martial Artist fearlessly grinned as he emerged from his hiding place in the casket.

"You sure took your time, Shisandan. I even managed to beat you here."

Ares was at a loss. He had come to the ruins with Danan, so his presence here didn't seem too impossible. However, this Danan was very different from the one that Ares had happened upon earlier. The burly man before him was missing his right forearm. Yet even so, he exuded a powerful presence that left Ares with no doubt that he was the real Danan.

It was then that Ares finally understood what had happened. The man he'd taken for Danan earlier was an Asura demon that had eaten Danan's flesh and assumed his form. The very same Asura demon that had approached him in the ruins.

"So you managed to survive. You've got the tenacity of a cockroach. I'll grant you that," Shisandan remarked.

"Ha-ha-ha. You probably mean that as an insult, but I respect their resilience. The way they cling to life is just another type of strength." Danan thrust his left arm out and slowly began inching closer. "Oy, Ares. This one's mine. Don't you dare butt in."

Shisandan's expression tensed as Danan approached. The man was practically emanating the thrill of battle from every pore.

The numbness in my hand won't disappear... A Martial Art?

That hurled sword had been thrown knowing that Shisandan would block it. The demon's fingers were trembling, keeping him from gripping his blade correctly. That left him unable to perform more than the clumsy swordsmanship of a beginner who had just picked up a weapon for the first time.

He got me. Letting both of my arms get disabled was foolish. Even if I change back to my original form, I won't be able to control them any better.

An Asura demon's natural shape had six arms, but damage taken while transformed didn't simply disappear if the creature reverted back. If one of Shisandan's arms was severed while he was Bui, it would be the same as having three of his actual arms cut off.

But he doesn't have his right arm, either. Can he really fight like that?

The moment Danan stepped into Shisandan's range, the one-armed Martial Artist and the Asura demon kicked off the ground. Shisandan brought his sword down, but Danan deflected it with his left hand. The next moment, Danan's arm whipped through the air, catching Shisandan straight in the face.

"Argh?!"

The demon stumbled backward several steps. He tried to ready his weapon again but slipped to one knee as if the strength had left his body.

"Oh yeah, before I forget," Danan said as he looked down on Shisandan. "I'm not gonna forgive you. In fact, I'm gonna beat the shit out of you till you're dead. But I do have to thank you."

"What?"

"You made me realize that I had been neglecting my left hand. I never knew I could use it so well if I just put my mind to it. It's made me even stronger than I was before."

Having seen Danan fight during their time traveling with Ruti, Ares could tell that was not a bluff.

Illogical as it was, this fighting fool had become even more powerful after losing his right arm.

*   *   *

The battle continued, Danan keeping the lead all the while. Shisandan loosed one attack after another, but his movements were sloppy. Both of his arms had been half-paralyzed because of the Martial Art: Horn-Breaker Fang-Smasher that Danan had sprung on him.

"Orahhh! You're full of openings! Trampling Kick!" An intense, energy-clad roundhouse slammed into Shisandan's stomach. His body flew into the air from the Martial Art's impact before slamming into the wall behind him and collapsing on hands and knees.

"Take this!"

There was ferocious grin on Danan's face as he unleashed a fearsome kick without giving Shisandan a chance to stand back up. It was all the demon could do to defend himself. He couldn't even manage a counterattack.

"Ares!" Shisandan shouted the Sage's name. It was clear what he wanted... He was asking for help.

"..." Ares did not aid him, however. At present, his thoughts were in complete disorder. *Me attack Danan, a man I have traveled together with for so long—one of the Hero's comrades? I can't do it, I can't, I can't...*

"Ares!" called Shisandan again.

Ares wanted to cover his ears and curl up into a ball. How lovely it would have been if he could forget everything around him.

Think! Act! Press forward and don't stop! You are wise. The choices you make are correct because you are the Sage.

The impulses of Ares's blessing drowned out his own feelings. Ares had no right to leave a decision to someone else. No matter the situation, he must think and act for himself, even if his blessing would not tell him the correct choice. The blessing screamed at him to behave in a manner befitting the Sage.

"Help me, Ares!" Shisandan cried for the third time. A flurry of blows rained down on the demon, drawing blood with every strike.

The shape-shifter will die before long, thought Ares. With that, he realized that if Shisandan met his end, Ares would never again be able to return to the Hero's party. *Well, I suppose there's nothing left to consider, then.*

"Gargantuan Storm Javelin!"

Danan was a simple man. He believed that Shisandan had deceived Ares just like the demon had deceived him. Thus, it seemed obvious that Ares would stand against the demon once he knew Shisandan's true identity. There was no doubt in Danan's mind. For as much as he disliked Ares, Danan still believed the Sage was a good person deep down. He'd been one of the Hero's comrades, after all.

"Wha—?! Ares?! The hell?!"

It was as if a storm large enough to cover an entire country had been compressed to a single black spear. The spell was of the highest order. Only the greatest Mage blessings had access to it.

Danan was slow to react to the unexpected attack, but he managed to twist his body with his supernatural reflexes, avoiding a direct hit. Unfortunately, even the electricity crackling around the javelin was enough to bathe Danan's body in energy that would have been enough to split a giant, centuries-old tree.

"Gaaaaaaaah!!!"

The beefy man's body locked up as tongues of lightning licked him. His vision went dark for a moment between the tremendous flash of light and intense pain. And in that split second, blood was spilled.

"Gh…"

Shisandan's sword was buried deep in Danan's side.

"Burst."

With that word, an explosion erupted from Shisandan's weapon. It tore the wound wide open, and the heat and explosive force shredded Danan's body from the inside.

"Even you can't survive a blast from inside your body."

However, Danan did not fall.

As if heedless of his own blood dripping to the floor, Danan clenched his fist and silently assumed a stance.

"Humans are truly fascinating. I've never seen a Martial Artist like you before. Your strength far surpasses the role of your blessing."

Shisandan stood slowly, signing a seal with his left hand. His body expanded, growing to almost two and a half meters tall. He had six muscular arms. His dark face transformed into that of a fanged Asura demon. Shisandan drew the five other swords at his waist, one after the other. This six-sword style was Asura demons' traditional combat style.

Danan took a single big step back, planted his right leg firmly, and faced the attack head-on. His eyes were hollow, but he had not lost the will to fight. The sextet of swords swirled like a tornado, crashing down in rapid succession. Every swing contained the strength to split Danan's enormous frame in two. Yet even covered in wounds and half unconscious, Danan met the cascade of blows with just his one arm and shattered each weapon.

It was said that Danan could tear steel with his fingers, and even on death's door, he lived up to that.

"You truly are a monster of martial arts, but—" Shisandan twisted his right leg like a snake. Danan was occupied blocking the storm of steel with just one arm, leaving him open as Shisandan's leg slammed into his chest.

"Gah! Hah…"

Pain coursed through Danan's chest. When Shisandan's leg

pulled back, the broken tip of a sword was protruding from where he'd kicked.

"I'm quite skilled at hand-to-hand combat myself. Though to you, it may seem little more than mere acrobatics," Shisandan remarked with a grin.

As he was kicking, Shisandan had grasped the broken sword point flying through the air with his toes and slammed it into Danan's chest in a single flowing strike.

"N...no...that was...real... It's my...loss..." Danan's lips cracked ever so slightly as he stared Shisandan down, bearing no grudge for Ares's intervention.

Finally reaching his limit, Danan collapsed.

*   *   *

Ares was surprised at how calm he felt after seeing Danan slump to the ground. He had raised his hand against a comrade, betrayed him. It seemed odd to Ares that he was not more shaken. Why did he not suffer from guilt?

I know why... I'm used to it. Because this isn't the first time I've turned on a comrade. Gideon's face flashed in the back of Ares's mind. *We really were together for a long time.*

Ares had joined the party after Ruti's arrival in the capital. He had been in the party the longest after Gideon and had adventured with Gideon more than anyone other than Ruti. They'd fought and survived countless battles, had flirted with death more times than could be counted, and had saved each other on more than a few occasions.

Ares hated Gideon, but he had also trusted in his ability. He may well have been the one who best understood just how amazing Gideon truly was.

Which was why I got rid of him.

With Gideon there, Ares could not live up to his blessing. Ruti would never come to trust him, and the other party members wouldn't rely on him. Gideon, even without skills, had been a far wiser man than he.

Ares finally understood the reason he had pushed Gideon away.

"Thanks for the help, Ares," the giant Asura demon remarked.

Ares had made his decision. He would walk with Shisandan, choosing the path of betrayal to reclaim the Hero who had been stolen from him. There was no more turning back.

"Let's keep going. It's up ahead, right? A relic of the Hero?"

"Indeed."

Ares left Danan on the ground there and continued farther into the ruins with Shisandan.

*   *   *

A powerful trap had been set just before the entrance to the deepest chamber. However, Shisandan pulled the heartstone from his cloak and sent his magic power into the ancient elf control board beside the door. In only a few minutes, the perilous device was disabled.

Ares could not imagine so powerful a trap being so easily controlled. Folk likened the precise magical control needed to operate the controls of ancient elf technology to hitting a fly's eye with an arrow, and for a good reason. Such thoughts immediately left Ares's mind when he saw what lay in the room, though. A golden box that had likely been made by wood elves.

"Th-that's...?!"

Five longswords rested in the radiant container. Ares immediately recognized them.

"Th-the Holy Demon Slayer?! B-but there are..."

The artifact-tier longsword that Ruti wielded—the Holy Demon Slayer. Bequeathed to the Hero by God and passed down to each subsequent bearer of the mightiest blessing. It was an invincible, sacred blade that had slain countless demon lords.

Somehow, there were five of this previously unique weapon in the golden box.

"No," Shisandan corrected him. "The Holy Demon Slayer is a replica of these swords. These are the first Hero's blades, taken from their grave. They are the original weapons bequeathed by God."

"Th-then these are the genuine articles?"

"Correct. To distinguish, perhaps I should call these True Avenger—no, Sacred Avenger."

Shisandan slid four of the five blades from the box into the empty sheaths hanging at his waist. The final one, he handed to Ares.

"At a fundamental level, the Hero blessing is as one with the replica Demon Slayer; they are God's reproductions of the first Hero's soul."

"Reproduced? Soul?"

"To make the current Hero fulfill their blessing, there are two things that must be done."

That was Ares's goal. He grasped the hilt that Shisandan held out to him. "And they are?"

"The first is to have her take the Sacred Avenger in her hand. Just as with the Holy Demon Slayer, these weapons have a power that magnifies the Divine Blessing of the Hero. If the blessing is boosted, the impulses will also increase. It should be enough to restore the urges suppressed by Devil's Blessing."

"Th-then Ruti will return to my side, right?!"

"No. That alone is not enough. At a fundamental level, the Hero is merely a vessel that serves as the manifestation of justice. The Hero experiences no fear, no doubt, and no hesitation. That is why those who bear that blessing experience impulses so powerful that they subsume the vessel's ego."

"Then what is the second requirement?" Ares pressed.

"Why has the current incarnation attempted to live life as 'Ruti' rather than 'the Hero'? It's because she has a desire that cannot be fulfilled unless she remains Ruti. She clings to a wish she longs to achieve, even in the face of suffering under her blessing's urges. It is necessary to remove the pillar of support to which she clings."

"...Gideon..."

Hearing Ares's whisper, Shisandan nodded in satisfaction.

*   *   *

Meanwhile, Gideon, or rather, Red, was with his comrades, chasing after Ares.

"I sense someone fighting in the distance."

Heeding Tisse's warning, the group quickened their pace. Not even Red could guess the path Ares had chosen.

Their confrontation could no longer be avoided.

Chapter 4

The Hero vs. The Sage

We hurried into the depths of the ruins. Ruti had not explored this deep, but the defensive clockwork golems weren't functioning, and there was nothing to get in our way. The corridors were filled with an eerie silence.

"H-hey, little missy," Godwin called out to Tisse pathetically. She spared him just a single glance. "I'm just gonna get in y'all's way, right? Wouldn't it be better I went outside to wait?"

"And you'd have me wait out there with you?"

"I mean, it's not like I can defend myself... I'm beggin' ya here. I can't see myself surviving if I stick around with you guys."

"There isn't any place safer than with us," Tisse declared flatly.

Godwin slumped in disappointment, but he obediently followed, not showing any sign of trying to run off into the ruins by himself.

Finally, we reached a vast hall of some sort. Magical lanterns were hanging from the ceiling, and three elevators stood ready to carry passengers deeper underground. At one point, a sign hung above them, but there was evidence that it had been forcibly torn away.

The tables and chairs around the hall had all been destroyed, as if a fit of rage had struck the wood elves who had made it this far. Ancient elven furniture was extraordinarily sturdy, so it wouldn't break without the use of magic or skills. I guess the appliances must have really bothered them. Perhaps they'd seen something here that set them off?

A *clank* issued from one of the elevators. A force field was engaged as ancient elf magic from time immemorial activated, accompanied by the sound of an elevator sliding up toward us.

"Shisandan." I started to draw my bronze sword, but before I could, a gleaming silver longsword appeared in front of me. Ruti was holding out my trusted old sword, Thunderwaker.

"You held on to it? I was sure you would have sold it."

"I would never do that. It's your sword."

I was a bit hesitant to take the weapon. It was a symbol of my time with the Hero's party, totally at odds with how I was currently living my life. Still, I grasped its hilt firmly. If Rit was ready to return to adventuring one last time to get her revenge, then I could go back to being Gideon for a bit, too.

"Thank you." I kept my words of gratitude short and performed a single practice swing to reaffirm my feel for Thunderwaker. It was entirely different from the bronze sword I used in Zoltan. The Weapon Proficiency: Longsword skill that remained dormant whenever I wielded my bronze sword activated again, and I could feel myself becoming one with the sword. "All right."

The elevator would soon arrive. There was another *clank* as the brakes engaged, and a single solid door slid open. What appeared was a man in armor with a shotel at his waist.

"It's been so long, my cute little disciple."

It was Gaius, the head of the royal guard in Loggervia and Rit's master.

"Shisandaaaaaan!!!"

Rit rushed forward with both shotels drawn.

"Wait! Something's off!"

Ruti's warning was too late, though. Rit was already swinging one of her swords at the figure standing in the elevator.

"?!"

The Gaius standing in the elevator didn't so much as twitch as Rit charged. Her blades caught nothing but empty air.

"An illusory decoy! His real body is…"

Shisandan was invisible, standing behind Rit as he drove a sword toward her back.

Surprisingly, Rit was smirking. If she knew an attack coming from behind, it didn't matter whether she could see her enemy or not. Just the sensation of menace in the air was enough for Rit to catch Shisandan's blade with the shotel in her right hand.

"I figured you would try that. There's no way I'd fall for such obvious provocation." Rit was still the same skilled fighter she had been during her adventuring days. Her left shotel sped toward Shisandan's legs.

"Red!"

"Got it!"

I brought my sword to bear on the Asura demon from behind. I'd realized Rit's plan as soon as she'd started running, and I had moved closer so that I could strike Shisandan when the moment was right. We didn't need words. I could understand what she was thinking.

Shisandan's invisibility ended when my blade met one of his, revealing the imposing figure of the Asura demon's true form. His legs were spread as he blocked Rit's strike as well.

"Tch." Shisandan made a displeased sound.

"What now, Asura demon? You set a trap for Rit, but only got yourself flanked," I said

"Then I guess it can't be helped! Heartstone! Unleash all your magic power!"

A torrent of water sprang up all around us.

"An undine's magic?!"

Rit and I were knocked back by the water. Thankfully, I controlled my landing with a roll and immediately sprang back to my feet. Rit was knocked into one of the elevators, but she was quickly back in a fighting stance, too.

Shisandan took a breath to regain his composure.

Just a little bit more, and our swords would have reached him. However, his desperate maneuver should have exhausted all the power in the magic item he'd used. Plus, he was still caught between the two of us. We still had the advantage.

Still though, are those wood elf swords? Seems odd for a demon to use such things. And those four still in the sheaths at his waist are bothering me.

Rit and I both kicked off the ground, unleashing another attack. However, no sooner had we done so than an uncomfortable premonition struck me.

"Magic?!"

I hastily switched to a defensive stance.

"Paralyzing Flame!"

One of the facades in the room disappeared, revealing a wall just behind it.

Creating a hidden space by casting an illusionary wall right in front of the true one, huh?

Poisonous flames erupted from the ground, racing toward Rit and me. The spell could stun you on contact. Neither Rit nor I had any resistance to paralysis. Rit could try to fight it using her spirit magic, and I could tough it out and resist because of my blessing's high level, but that would only work if the enemy was at a similar level. It turned out our new opponent was the pinnacle of human mages; his magic would be nigh impossible to resist.

"Ares!"

The one who had loosed the spell was none other than Ares the Sage. At his waist was another one of the swords that Shisandan kept at his, for a total of five.

Has he lost his mind and joined up with a demon?!

"Die, Gideon!"

The flames drew closer, but a radiant white shell of light surrounded us.

"Sacred Magic Shield." Ruti cast a spell with her left hand.

Trained through thousands of battles with the demon lord's forces, she had anticipated the possibility of Ares betraying us and had remained where she was standing, at the ready. "This is your last chance, Ares. Surrender now, and I can still let you walk away," she cautioned.

"There is still time, Ruti. Please just say that you will continue the Hero's journey together with me," Ares replied, seemingly oblivious to her statement.

Both quickly began to work new spells.

"Gargantuan Storm Javelin!"

"Sacred Punisher."

A tempestuous black javelin and lightning that brought divine judgment took shape. The Sage and the Hero's greatest spells clashed, and the aftermath was enough that Shisandan, Rit, and I all had to stop fighting for a moment. The tremendous impact was enough to send cracks through the floor, walls, and ceiling.

"So we're equal in magic," Ruti murmured.

Neither spell overcame the other. Both dispersed at the same time.

It was hard to say whether Ares deserved praise for matching the Hero or if I should be dumbfounded that Ruti, a frontline fighter, could use magic on par with a Sage.

If there were more people like Ruti around, mages would be entirely worthless.

This was a battle between two who had surpassed what normal humans could.

"L-leave me the hell out of thiiiiiiiiis!!!" Godwin started running, a look of terror on his face. "I don't have any dog in this fight! Heroes should just stick to fighting one another and not trouble themselves with me!"

Someone like Godwin could easily get blown away as collateral damage in this fight. He had finally had enough and started sprinting for the exit in a panic.

"Wait! Don't run!" I frantically called out to him, but there was no reasoning with him in such a state.

"Arise, great fangs and grand wings! Come, lord of beasts! Summon Spirit Drake!" Ares smirked as he activated his magic. Just when Godwin was about to escape the room, magic power swirled right before him, forming an enormous figure.

"Eek?!" The man fell backward and shrieked as a green-scaled creature took shape in front of him. The spirit drake Ares had summoned opened its toothy jaws and began to approach Godwin.

Not good. If I tried to help, however, Rit would be pinned down by Shisandan! I was stuck!

"Gyaaaaagh?!"

Thankfully, Godwin did not end up becoming fodder for the drake. A throwing knife pierced the beast's right eye and caused it to recoil and screech in pain.

"As I said, the safest place you can be is at our side, so please just behave yourself." Tisse had thrown the dagger. Her expression was unchanged as she stood between Godwin and the drake.

"A-are you sure?! You realize that's a freaking drake, right?!" Godwin asked nervously.

Perhaps the sight of such a small girl opposing the large creature left Godwin feeling doubtful. Even I had to admit, when one considered scale alone, Tisse seemed the clear loser.

"Indeed, my blessing is not well suited to this sort of situation," admitted Tisse.

"Th-then—!" Godwin stammered.

"It will take me a full minute."

Naturally, there was no way that Tisse would lose to a spirit drake. The only hang-up was that, excluding Godwin, she would be the slowest to defeat it one-on-one. The Assassin blessing had many skills for seizing upon advantageous situations. Fighting while guarding another was not one of its specialties. Even so, Tisse was far stronger than the highest-tier spirit beast.

There was a powerful confidence in her words, leaving Godwin speechless as he watched Tisse in awe from his seat on the ground.

*   *   *

So far it's going according to plan…!

Ruti was alone now, just as Ares wanted. With her comrades distracted, she was facing off against Ares by herself.

The feeling of Ruti's hostility focused solely on him was like an icy dagger in the heart. Yet at the same time, he felt an odd sense of exaltation.

Ruti hasn't made any real moves yet. She wants to protect that Alchemist, but now he and Tisse have moved toward the exit. With them spread out like this, it will be difficult for her to guard everyone from my magic. In which case, she should charge in with her sword. She obviously knows I could use a spell on Gideon before she gets in close. But if I did that, I wouldn't be able to protect myself, and she will assume that I want to keep myself safe.

Ares's right hand touched the Sacred Avenger.

But that is actually what I want. If Shisandan is to be believed, if I draw this sword and it touches her body, the Hero blessing will be enhanced. Then she should realize that working together with me is the most effective way of achieving her destiny and will become a nonfactor in this battle. If Ruti is the Hero, then it will be impossible for her to turn against me!

So long as Ruti didn't intervene, the rest were little more than annoyances. If it had been Danan, Theodora, and Yarandrala, Ares would have been warier, but he was facing the dropouts Gideon and Rit and the placeholder Tisse. Ares was sure of his victory.

*   *   *

Rit and I were attacking Shisandan from both sides.

He's stronger than the last time we fought.

Even though we had the advantage of flanking him, once he was able to steady himself, he managed to continue deflecting our combined barrage. The demon was not the sort of opponent who would go down quickly, but we couldn't afford to be taking our time, either.

I was worried about Ruti. She was facing off against Ares alone. Normally, Ares would have no hope of winning, but none understood that better than him. Undoubtedly, he had some sort of plan.

"What are those swords you and Ares are carrying, Shisandan?" I demanded.

"Oh? I should have expected as much from you, Gideon. Worried, are you?" Shisandan seemed genuinely impressed. "You'll find out soon enough," he appended with a grin.

The next instant, everyone in the room felt the chill of death approaching. We forgot our respective battles for a split second and instinctively looked over at Ruti.

"Martial Art: Great Whirlwind."

Using the tremendous strength of her blessing, Ruti swung her sword with great force and speed in a spinning slash. A shock wave raced, leaving deep gouges in the walls. Perhaps because of the Hero's strength, the cut she loosed did not have any effect on us, but her enemies were consumed in a whirlwind of strikes.

"E-eeeeeeep!" Godwin screamed as the spirit drake's head was severed and rolled toward him before disappearing in a burst of light.

"To think she had grown so strong," Shisandan exclaimed.

All six of the elven blades he had used to defend himself shattered, and his lower two arms were hanging limply, drenched in blood.

"Agh, ahhh..."

Ares had managed to escape uninjured. From the looks of it, he had hurriedly defended himself with the sword at his waist. However, the weapon had been shattered into pieces, leaving just a broken hilt in his hand.

"Th-that's impossible." Ares's voice was quivering.

Was that blade his trump card for dealing with Ruti? I wondered.

Up until that, Shisandan had remained composed throughout our exchange, but now his expression was tense. After taking a short breath, though, the demon's placid look returned.

"Ares, I'll deal with Ruti. You keep going."

"Huh? Ah. Right."

"I hadn't counted on her breaking the sword, but I had expected you to fail. It will be fine." Shisandan stomped his foot down with a thud.

"What's this? Not looking so hot now, are you, Shisandan?" This time, I was provoking him. It would be nice if he would let that take him out of his groove, but there was no way he would be that easy an opponent.

"Indeed, I have to admit that your sister is a truly dangerous being. All the more reason though that she cannot be allowed to become anything other than the Hero."

"What is that supposed to mean?"

Shisandan and I stared each other down.

"Watch out!" Tisse shouted. "Something is coming from below!"

"Below?! Not good! Rit! Run!"

"Huh?"

I was about to dash over to Rit, but Shisandan stood in my way.

"Out of my way!" I swung Thunderwaker down at the demon standing there with two wounded arms and all his swords broken. Unfortunately, he met my slash with a radiant longsword he drew from one of the scabbards at his hip.

"Wha—?! The Holy Demon Slayer?!"

For an instant, my attention was drawn to his sword. It was no more than a fraction of a second, but that moment of lost time was irreplaceable.

The floor of the elevator Rit was in burst upward.

"A second spirit drake?!"

A spirit drake wearing full-body armor had burst into the cramped elevator, mouth wide as it menaced Rit. Off-balance, Rit kicked against the wall, forcing herself to remain standing as she slashed the drake's face with her shotel.

Even in such a situation, Rit should have been able to fight off the drake. When she saw its rider, however, she went stiff.

"Y-you?!"

"Holy Chains."

"Wha—?! Nrgh?!"

Rit's body was bound by radiant metal links. It was an extraordinarily powerful clerical art that not even Rit could escape.

"Theodora?! Why?!"

The woman atop the spirit drake ignored Rit's cry and leaped out of the shaft, her spear at the ready. Sensing this new trouble, Ruti dashed to the elevator. Theodora's spear and Ruti's blade clashed, and the two of them came to a stop.

"Why?" Ruti asked. She seemed unable to believe what she was seeing.

"For the sake of this world. Hate me if you will. I will slit my stomach in atonement when this is done. But right now, your sacrifice is necessary for this world!"

Ruti hesitated at the words. Though she was superior in strength, Theodora was still managing to hold her back.

"Why me? Why must I be sacrificed for the world?"

"Because you are the Hero."

"I never asked to be! Countless other people dream of becoming a hero and saving the world! So why does it have to be me?!" Ruti steeled herself, ducking beneath Theodora's swipe and stepping firmly in toward the Crusader with a thrust aimed at her armored torso. Ruti's attacks were mighty enough to pierce dragon scales, but Theodora twisted her body and dexterously avoided a direct hit. There was a metallic screech from her armor as Ruti's sword scraped past.

Just like Danan, Theodora was a master of her style. There were not many people on the continent capable of evading Ruti while wearing armor.

"If you don't fight, an untold number of people will die."

Theodora drew her polearm back. Short blades adorned each side of the spearhead, and Theodora was using them to aim for Ruti's back. Ruti ducked and, without even looking, knocked the incoming slash aside using the armored gauntlet encasing her hand.

"What?!"

It was an absurd defense that did not exist in any standard style of swordsmanship. Only one with superhuman physical abilities could pull it off. Even Theodora could not react to such an unpredictable maneuver. Her stance broke from the excess momentum of swinging her spear. Using that opening, Ruti moved out of range.

"Why do I have to sacrifice myself to save the lives of countless people I've never even met before?"

"Because that is God's will."

Both of their voices were wrung out and strained.

The Hero would have had no trouble with suffering for others, but Ruti was the one fighting now. She far outclassed Theodora. The only reason they were fighting on remotely even terms was that Theodora's words had dulled Ruti's prowess.

"Dammit!"

I wanted to dash over to Ruti in order to take her place fighting Theodora. It pained me not to stand in front of my sister and shield her from the woman's biting words, but...

"Rit!"

Rit was still in the elevator, bound by Theodora's magic and grasped by the spirit drake's claws.

"Heh-heh-heh, two people to be saved—your lover and your little sister. It must be difficult to decide, Gideon."

Shisandan's tusked mouth warped in laughter. The Asura demon was still staring me down. If I turned my back and rushed to Ruti, Shisandan would easily finish off Rit, and if I wanted to save Rit, I would have to get past him. Despite possessing no blessing, Shisandan was strong. Even fighting together with Rit, we hadn't managed to get through his defenses.

I unleashed a storm of feints and slashes, but he easily parried my blade with the holy sword he was wielding. Strong didn't begin to describe this creature. While two of his arms were disabled, something had changed the moment he'd drawn one of those four blades. The aura around him had swelled, and now he seemed entirely different.

I had no clue whether what he held was a real Holy Demon Slayer, but there was no doubt it was an exceptional magical sword. If I met it head on with Thunderwaker, my weapon wouldn't come out unscathed.

While I was struggling, I glanced over at Theodora.

"This is reality. Sir Gideon is one of the finest swordsmen in the world, but without the Hero, even he is unable to save his love. Humanity needs you to fulfill your destiny."

Ruti's expression was racked with pain.

Goddammit! My jaw went tight.

I was on the verge of losing myself in rage at the thought that my struggles were making Ruti suffer.

Yet just as I was about to snap, there came a thunderous *slam* from the elevator. Still bound by Theodora's chains, Rit had kicked the spirit drake's head back into the wall.

"Who asked you?" Rit cried, leveling a seething gaze straight at Theodora. "What gives you the right to put my life in the hands of the Hero?!" She was furious. Vehemently, ferociously enraged.

Still staggered, the drake tried to clamp down on Rit again, but she kicked its head straight up. The beast's head slammed into the ceiling before slumping back down. The elevator floor had been left in poor shape after the spirit drake had crashed through, and there was hardly any sound footing. With her arms bound, Rit could not use her swords or magic. That hardly seemed to matter to Rit, however, as she turned to stare Theodora down.

"But it was the Hero who saved your homeland, was it not? Are you not proof yourself that the Hero is necessary to save the world?" countered Theodora.

"You're wrong!"

"How?"

"It wasn't the Hero or the Guide or a Crusader who saved Logger-via or me." Rit struck the drake's head a third time with her foot. Broken teeth went flying. "It was Ruti, Red, and you, Theodora! You're the ones who rescued us!"

"...A distinction without difference."

"It's not the same at all! A hero isn't some class of blessing. It's how we describe people! Loggervia wasn't saved by the mere presence of a blessing! It was because you—all of you—urged us to stand back up. That was what delivered Loggervia from evil! I thought you at least would understand that much, even if Ares can't!"

"I am merely a servant of Almighty Demis... What other choice do I have?!" demanded Theodora.

"Anyone who would force another to bear the fate of the world against their will is wrong, and if that's really the will of God, then God's wrong, too, and I'll say it to his face if I have to!" Rit screamed.

Both Ruti and Theodora froze in shock at that.

"Fascinating. Humans truly are fascinating," Shisandan mur-mured as he locked swords with me. "That's it precisely. A hero is not merely born. Only those who *strive to be* a hero are worthy of the title. And yet God, in his foolishness, cannot even comprehend that much."

"What...?" I managed through clenched teeth. Strangely, it felt like Shisandan was expressing genuine admiration for Rit's statement.

"Alas, though, we are enemies." The Asura demon lifted a leg.

"Rit! Look out!"

Shisandan dexterously kicked a fragment of one of the elven swords lying on the ground at her. It was a precise shot, stabbing straight into her left thigh.

"Argh!"

Crimson liquid seeped down her leg and stained the ground.

"Finish her, creature!" Shisandan commanded.

The spirit drake's mouth bore down on Rit from above. Her arms were bound, and her leg was wounded. Seeing that, I finally snapped.

"Rit!!!" I abandoned all defense, loosing an attack with every bit of my power, but Shisandan just slipped aside, yielding the path to Rit without a clash. Cold sweat poured down my back.

A trap?!

I had been lured in. I was playing into Shisandan's hands now. Still, I didn't care.

"Thunderwaker! Pierce my foe!"

I dove into the elevator as I thrust my sword, stabbing straight through the spirit drake's neck and up through its head. Immediately, the beast went limp. No longer able to maintain itself in this realm, its body faded away.

I grabbed Rit and was about to leap back out when I saw Ares grinning victoriously. Tisse hurled two knives to interrupt his magic, but he guarded his face with his left arm, content to let the daggers hit his limb. There was a spray of blood, but the thrill of his triumph seemed to keep him from noticing any pain.

"This is it! Iron Wall!"

The roof of the elevator Rit and I were in began to creak. Ares had conjured an enormous lump of metal on top of our elevator. The sound I heard was that of the tether giving way under a load far beyond anything it could support.

"Run, Red!" Rit screamed.

My Lightning Speed meant that I could get out in time on my own. That would mean letting go of Rit, though…

Maybe that would have been the right thing to do. Us both plummeting wouldn't help anyone. I wondered if I would've been able to make the optimal choice back when I was still Gideon.

"Sorry, Rit."

But I wasn't Gideon anymore. I was Red. Taking up Thunderwaker again hadn't changed that. Even knowing I wouldn't make it, I wasn't going to let go of Rit.

"Big Brother!!!"

Whatever hesitation had been holding Ruti back vanished in an instant. Theodora's spear was suddenly cleaved in two. Whirling gracefully, Ruti stepped into a lunge, thrusting her sword through Theodora's armor.

"As expected of the Hero... This is why I..."

Theodora, one of humanity's greatest practitioners of clerical arts and a true master of the spear, fell to the ground. She had only held Ruti back a short while, but it had been decisive.

Before Ruti could reach it, the elevator gave way, and Rit and I were dropped into the dark.

"I finally win! At last, Gideon loses!" Ares shouted jubilantly.

Chapter 5
- - - - - - - - -
The Guide

The Divine Blessing of the Hero had been suppressing Ruti's emotions since the day she was born. Even at level 1, she had Immunity to Fear. As such, Ruti had never known what it really meant to feel afraid.

"AAAAAAAAAAAAAAAAAAAH!!!!!!" For the first time in her life, a terrible shriek of terror clawed its way from her throat.

The person she loved most in the world was going to die right before her eyes. She would never be able to see him again. Never be able to hear him say her name again. Never be able to feel his warmth again. She'd finally started growing able to express how she felt and had been looking forward to enjoying an unexciting and slow life with the one she loved. Yet it had all ended before it ever truly began.

Something shattered inside Ruti. The thing that had supported her throughout the living hell that was her life crumbled.

"Yes." As Ruti stared in a daze, Shisandan swung the four Sacred Avengers at her. "You, not the Hero, are shaken by Gideon's death. In this one moment, I am stronger than you. It was all for this one moment!"

Even in her current state, though, Ruti met Shisandan's attack with the Holy Demon Slayer, precisely fending off his strike. The screech of sacred blades clashing resounded throughout the chamber.

"Breaking Ares's Sacred Avenger with your reproduction was truly an act worthy of praise. You may be the strongest bearer of the Hero's blessing to ever live. Sadly, that power is not without a price." As if timed to the Asura demon's words, Ruti's Holy Demon Slayer snapped in half. "Your sword was already on death's door after that attack."

Shisandan spun his four weapons, slicing the floor around the two of them. Ruti stared at her broken sword with hollow eyes as she and Shisandan fell.

*   *   *

"Kh. Heh-heh. Ah-ha-ha-ha-ha-ha-ha-ha-ha!!!" Ares was laughing uncontrollably. "I won! With this, I can continue the journey with Ruti! See?! I'm superior to Gideon! This is the proof! He's dead, and I'm alive! The winner and the loser! The Sage and the fool! Ah-ha-ha-ha-ha-ha-ha-ha!!!"

As he cackled gleefully, Ares moved his right hand in an arcane motion.

"Tornado Cutter!"

A vortex made of razor-like air surged to life. Its gales deflected the knives Tisse hurled at Ares, sending them straight back at the Assassin.

"Aaaaagh!!!" Tisse collapsed to the ground in a puddle of her own blood as the shredding wind surrounding her faded.

"Turning on your client? I should have expected as much from an honorless killer for hire," Ares derided.

"…Why?" wheezed Tisse, her voice growing weak.

"Hmm?"

"You were in love with Ms. Ruti. How could you do this?"

"What do you mean? She's the Hero."

Ares's reply made it clear that he believed any sacrifice would be forgiven if it was for the greater good of helping Ruti live up to her blessing. That was the best thing for the Hero and the greatest gift one could give to her.

Tisse grit her teeth and forced herself up, even as crimson still flowed from her injuries. Shaking, she drew her shortsword.

"Ohhh, that's quite remarkable. I doubt I'd be able to stand in your condition. Sadly, you suffer in vain. If you had just stayed down, this could have ended without your death. Assuming you didn't perish from blood loss," Ares remarked coldly.

Entrust Ms. Ruti to this man? Never. Even if Demis forgives him, I never will. Even if she is the Hero, she's my friend first and foremost. She's really, really strong, but she's also awkward and just slightly off...and she can fall in love. She's just a normal girl! I can't entrust my friend to a man who can't even understand that much!

Sadly, despite her intentions, Tisse's body collapsed against her will. Seeing that, Ares smirked.

Tears of regret streaked down Tisse's face. Watching her sob helplessly, witnessing her in such a state, *he* rose to stand before Ares.

"Hmm?"

A little spider leaped out of Tisse's bag and barred Ares's way, raising both of his front legs. His enemy was overwhelmingly strong, and he had no comrades to stand beside him. There was no chance he could win.

But what of it?! Mister Crawly Wawly put his small body in the path of the villain who had hurt his friend. And seeing that tiny figure's bravery, the last person in the room rose, too.

"Grahhhhhh! Piss off!" Godwin roared as he threw the thunderstone and smoke wand. An explosion sounded, and a thick cloud of vapor enveloped Ares.

Godwin had no idea what, if any, meaning there was in this battle. The man had been dragged to these ruins and kept here against his will. There were so many things wrong with this situation that he couldn't even count them all. Not too long ago, he had been trying

to run away, yet now he found himself standing to fight. Internally, he was still screaming "Why me?!" though.

As Bighawk's right-hand man, Godwin had done terrible things to a lot of people. He had allied with a demon to create a dangerous drug and played a large role in spreading the substance around Zoltan. Villain that he was, Godwin still held a set of principles, warped though they likely were. There were some lines no one was meant to cross!

"I'm a bad guy, but...I can't forgive a goddamn maniac delusional enough to convince himself he isn't evil!" Godwin howled. His teeth were chattering in terror, yet he drew a dagger that emanated darkness.

Ares beheld this latest development with clear exasperation. "Worthless scum. This is why I can't stand idiots. Force Shot."

The spell blew away the magic shadow and hurled Godwin into a wall, where he collapsed in a heap. Ares glanced at the motionless Alchemist. After confirming he was no longer a threat, Ares raised his leg and stomped down on Mister Crawly Wawly, who was still waving both of his front legs.

"You never had any hope of victory."

There was no one left to oppose him. All that remained was to listen to Gideon's final screams as he was crushed to a wretched pulp beneath the weight of the elevator and iron wall.

*　　　　*　　　　*

The elevator was approaching the bottom floor. In just a few more seconds, Red and Rit would die.

"Hahhhhhhhh."

Covered in wounds, the towering man focused his whole consciousness into his remaining arm. An elevator was barreling down toward him, but he didn't so much as spare it a passing look. In his mind, he envisioned all his strength gathering in a single point, then he forced that power up and out through his arm.

"I don't get all that complicated stuff—what Theodora was thinking, what the Hero was thinking, what's right, what's wrong. I can't be bothered to understand that crap."

Danan clenched his fist. Fresh blood began to seep as wounds he'd closed with a cure potion burst open again.

"But I can tell you this for sure!"

Calling upon everything he could muster, a lifetime of training, Danan thrust his fist upward.

"Martial Art: Rising Dragon's Roar!"

A dragon burst forth from his left arm. It was Danan's finisher, the technique he had used to blow a hole in a pirate galley and send it to the bottom of the sea. The dragon pierced the elevator, shattered the giant mass of iron, and continued climbing.

"Gideon! Rit! You're my friends! I'm not gonna let you die on me! That's a guarantee! I won't let anyone tell me different!"

*   *   *

"Danan?!"

When Theodora lost consciousness, the holy chains binding Rit had disappeared, but even with full access to both our skills, we didn't have a way of escaping the falling elevator. I had just about given up when a dragon made of energy pierced through the floor and blew through the heavy load over our heads.

"Get ready, Rit!" I called, still somewhat astonished.

"Got it!"

Carried by the dragon, we stood back-to-back and used our swords to deflect all the metal fragments raining down around us.

"Danan always comes through when it counts!" Rit exclaimed.

We clung to the dragon as we raced toward the upper floor.

*   *   *

Back in the fight, Rit and I jumped from our unlikely mount out of the shaft that had nearly been our grave.

"Ares!"

We'd only been absent for a few moments, but the hall was utterly transformed. Shisandan and Ruti were gone. There was a hole in the floor, so I assumed they'd gone down through it. Theodora was collapsed on the floor near the elevator, unconscious. Tisse and Godwin hardly looked any better. Mister Crawly Wawly lay injured at Ares's feet. It seemed he had fought, too.

Left arm still bleeding, Ares stared wide-eyed at me, his gaze filled with tangible hatred.

"Why?! How do you manage to survive with that useless blessing?!"

I took off sprinting toward Ares. The only hope I had of besting the Ultimate Mage was getting in close.

"Die! Die! Die, you bastard! Die! Gargantuan Storm Javelin!!!" With an arcane flourish, Ares hurled the conjured electrified lance straight at us.

"Gh?!"

It's too fast, I won't be able to dodge it! I gritted my teeth in preparation. The only thing to do was to meet the attack and push through.

"Spirit of the wind! Grant thine blessing and reject misfortune! Breath of Wind!"

Wind elementals danced in the air around me in response to Rit's call. The powerful javelin crashed into us, followed by violent thunder and a buffeting gale.

"Ghhhhhhhh!!!"

Rit's spirit magic couldn't totally counter Ares's spell, but it had weakened the impact enough to keep us from passing out.

Behind me, Rit was knocked back, and I could hear her roll

across the floor. There was no sign of her getting back up. She had poured all her strength into protecting me, leaving nothing to guard herself.

I resisted the urge to tend to her. Doing so would just waste the opening she had endangered herself to give me. However, leaving her was far greater agony than Ares's attack.

Only three steps separated me from Ares now. Just a little farther, and my sword would reach him. I couldn't give him the chance to use more magic!

∗   ∗   ∗

Fool. While he had suffered some setbacks, Ares still felt assured of his victory.

I gained an even more powerful skill after you were gone, Gideon. One that only a Sage can learn. Successive Activation allows me to cast a mystic art and clerical art one after the other using alternate hands. I've already got an instant-death spell ready and waiting for you. That pathetic blessing of yours doesn't have any resistances to instant-death attacks. Without Rit's spirit magic, you're naught but a paper tiger! I admit that your guile has proven vexing, but even you can't deal with a skill you don't know about! Our battle ends here!

Ares extended his left arm, Tisse's knife still sticking from it, and prepared to loose the spell that would finally do away with the biggest thorn in his side. However, his pointer finger moved in a way that he had not intended. The magic seal Ares was forming became disrupted, and the spell failed.

"What?!?!" Furious, Ares whirled to find Tisse lying in a puddle of blood with a grin on her face.

"Don't underestimate my friend!"

Mister Crawly Wawly had spun a thread around Ares's finger, and Tisse had pulled it. Red hadn't known about Successive Activation, but she had. She had been waiting for this moment.

Mister Crawly Wawly was no common spider. He and Tisse had grown stronger and closer together. He possessed the Divine Blessing of the Warrior. While one of the lowest-tier blessings, capable of nothing more than simple physical buffs, it was enough to keep the arachnid alive after being stepped on.

Mister Crawly Wawly had not leaped out without a plan. He had endured Ares's boot to wind that thread around the man's finger.

"B-but I couldn't possibly have missed that!"

Usually, Ares would indeed have been able to sense what Mister Crawly Wawly was doing since he was so much weaker relative to the Sage.

"Heh, heh-heh..." Godwin laughed listlessly from where he lay. "...Riskin' my life for a damn spider... Damn, this is a low point for me..."

The thunderstone, smoke wand, and his seemingly futile resistance had all been a distraction so that Ares wouldn't catch wise to Mister Crawly Wawly.

"Aaaaaaaaaaaaaaaaaagh!!!"

With Red closing in, Ares desperately tried to cast another spell.

Tisse, Godwin, and Mister Crawly Wawly had risked themselves to buy time, yet all it had won was a single extra second. Regardless, the three of them believed that brief moment to be enough. They trusted that it would be enough time for Red to win.

*   *   *

My Thunderwaker severed Ares's right hand midway through it preparing to cast a spell.

"Uwaaaaaaaaaaaaaaah!!!"

Ignoring Ares's screams, I lopped off his left hand, too.

"Forming a seal with your hand is a fundamental requirement to activate magic! Your magic is useless now!" I declared.

"Ahhhhhh! Arrrrrrrrrrrgh!!!"

Two strokes of my sword was all it took to rob the man of everything that defined him as a Sage.

"It's over now, Ares." I raised my weapon. There was just one final blow left to deal.

"S-save me! Shisandan! He's going to kill me! Theodora! Give me my hands back! Someone! Someone save me! Please, help!" Ares slumped to the floor, writhing and begging for aid. But there was no one left to answer Ares's call. "Wh-why?! Why is it always you?! I'm stronger! Wiser! Why did everyone choose you?!"

"You really haven't figured it out?" I asked.

Ares looked at me, eyes filled with despair. "P-please, spare me. I—I was just trying to be the Sage, Gideon... I was... I was just..."

"No more."

Thunderwaker sped down with all my strength behind it. The sword cleaved down from one shoulder through to the opposite hip, splitting Ares diagonally. He coughed up blood.

"M-my...dream..." Ares's words burbled through his bloody lips as he stretched his still-bleeding limbs toward the ceiling, as if reaching after something none but he could see. Godwin, Mister Crawly Wawly, Tisse, Rit, and I all watched in silence. With a gruesome sound, he hacked up more crimson liquid. "...Father..."

There was an almost childlike innocence to his voice as he went limp.

Ares the Sage was dead.

*   *   *

Danan shuddered feebly. He had used up all his strength. Seeing that, Albert frantically moved from outside the elevator shaft to support him.

"Are you okay, sir?"

Danan took the Extra Cure potion Albert offered, his last one, and downed it in a single gulp. The wounds covering his body closed back up. Massive, grotesquely colored bruises dotted Danan's body. He had suffered incredible internal trauma that Healer magic alone would not be able to resolve.

"I'm just a little tired 's all," said the Martial Artist.

"Any normal person would have been long since dead. And cure potions can't bring back the blood you lost," Albert remarked.

"It's just blood. All I've gotta do is eat some meat to get more of the stuff." Danan reached into his cloak and pulled out some jerky, but Albert anxiously stopped him.

"You can't! Your organs are all shredded, remember? Look, the elevator is here. We should head up."

The central elevator had been thoroughly destroyed, but the left and right ones were still functioning. While Danan was busy saving Red and Rit, Albert had been frantically messing with the control panel and had somehow managed to call an elevator.

"Tch, normally I'd just run straight up a shaft like this."

"…Without any magic…?"

Albert helped Danan into the elevator.

"I don't get what Theodora was doing at all. She chose to side with Ares and Shisandan but still wants you to save me. That woman's all over the place. I thought she was just bluffing to keep my surviving a secret, but I don't think that was it."

Back in the casket room, Theodora had inconspicuously confirmed that Danan was still alive and then promised to help Ares and Shisandan. The declaration had surprised Ares, but he was happy that someone finally seemed to understand his grand designs. It was Theodora who had suggested he and Shisandan head for the hall.

While that was happening, Albert, who Theodora had made invisible via magic, had waited until they were all gone and then given Danan a cure potion and administered some basic first aid.

"Indeed… If I had to guess, I'd say Ms. Theodora doesn't understand it herself, either. Her actions were contradictory because she was conflicted and didn't know what she wanted," Albert stated.

"Nothing makes any sense!" Danan scowled, conveying a deep

dissatisfaction. "If she really did stand against the Hero, then she's already dead."

"Really? Ms. Theodora is exceptionally capable, though," replied Albert.

"She is. She, Ares, and I are all strong enough to take on a few thousand soldier demons alone and win. But the Hero is leagues past us."

"...She's that strong?"

"If they fought, Theodora would have no chance of winning. Even if it was me, Ares, Theodora, Yarandrala, and Red, we'd still lose outright."

Albert looked uneasy. He realized the reason Danan was so bothered was that he was certain Theodora was dead.

Perhaps sensing Albert's tension, Danan whispered, "Sorry, if I could move just a little more, I could have carried you with me up one of the shafts. We'd have been there in no time."

✳　　　　　✳　　　　　✳

There was a metallic clang.

Ruti, clad in armor, slammed into the floor without so much as an attempt to control her tumble.

"..."

Shisandan landed nimbly, but Ruti was unconcerned with the creature. She blankly stared up at the hole in the ceiling above her. The Asura demon readied his four Sacred Avengers.

"So how do you feel, Hero?"

"Why? All I wanted was to live in peace with my brother."

"So the ego is still intact."

Ruti was not looking at Shisandan. Were she the Hero, her gaze would have been fixed on the demon, ready to smite him.

"Ruti the Hero, you truly are a grievous threat. As an Asura demon, I must slay you here."

Shisandan gripped his weapons tight. The glow of the Sacred Avengers intensified as a powerful strength flowed into Shisandan.

"You are strong. But the Sacred Avengers were holy swords created to slay beings like you. And with an Asura wielding them, there is no way they will fail!"

Though his opponent was an unarmed girl, Shisandan made no effort to hold back. He leaped forward, all four of his blades poised to strike. However, Ruti slowly rose to her feet and fended off Shisandan's attack with her broken holy sword.

"Grahhhhhhhhh!!!" Shisandan roared, and the brilliance coming off his weapons intensified. Finally, one of his strikes found purchase on Ruti's left arm. The girl pulled black, bleeding from the cut.

"...Is it really such a crime for me to live a normal life...?" she asked.

"How ironic that the blessing designed to prevent this very sort of situation ended up fostering the mental fortitude needed to endure its impulses. Yes, you must live as the Hero. Such is what the world demands."

"The world?"

"Admittedly, we Asura bear some responsibility for your current situation. I won't deny we've done a terrible thing to you. We had no choice but to defeat the previous demon lord and take the throne. No one, including God himself, will accept the Hero abandoning her duty and living in peace."

Ruti could not understand what Shisandan was saying. She threw her broken sword down with a clatter. "I never once asked for this. I don't want this strength."

"Pick up the sword," demanded the demon.

Ruti's left hand hung limp. She shuddered as if cowering from the very air around her.

Shisandan tossed one of his blades before the young woman. "Take up your sword, Ruti the Hero."

However, she didn't so much as glance at it.

"This terrible feeling in my chest. It's thanks to you that I'm able to remember it after so long. Wrath… Rage."

Shisandan steadied himself. Readying his three holy blades, he charged Ruti, intending to sever her head from her neck the moment he was close enough.

That power… Even if Devil's Blessing was the impetus, to think she would have manifested it so clearly. I have a duty as an Asura and as one who wields these swords. She must be stopped now.

Long ago, Red had taught Ruti the Bahamut Knights' style of swordsmanship. Using that as a base, she had developed her own form—a way of fighting unique to the Hero. However, practiced stances and motions were the furthest things from Ruti's mind at present. She wanted nothing more than to vent all the savage emotions swirling in her heart.

Slowly, she pulled her right hand back. "Give. Me. Back. My. Brother. And. My. Life." Ruti put her burning fury into her words, verbalizing the feeling that had driven her into such a blind frenzy. All that remained was to blow everything away.

From Shisandan's point of view, the girl vanished.

How can she move so quickly?! The demon hurried to assume a defensive position. *Swift or not, she's fighting bare-handed. I need only meet her attack with my swords and cut her down!*

Shisandan crossed his swords in front of him to catch Ruti's incoming attack.

"Kh-AAAAAAAAAAAAAAAAAAAAAAAAAAAAAAAH!!!!!"

For the first time in her life, young woman let out a battle cry. The ever calm and collected Hero was gone. This was Ruti.

"…How…?"

In an instant, it was over.

Strength drained from Shisandan's arms, and the swords in his hands slipped to the floor. Ruti's fist had completely shattered all three of the holy blades bequeathed to the first Hero by God.

"Gh…"

Thick, red liquid spilled from Shisandan's mouth. He pressed a trembling hand to his lips.

This is…a fatal wound…

Typically, the Asura demon would have pressed a hand against the injury to help staunch the flow of blood, but even with all six of his arms, he wouldn't have been able to cover the giant hole blown through his stomach.

Still, she touched the Sacred Avengers. At the very least, that is a victory. A satisfied smile crossed Shisandan's face as he collapsed. The Asura demon did not move again. He was dead.

✻   ✻   ✻

"That should do it."

I fished the fragments of Theodora's armor out of her wound and then had her drink a cure potion. That was enough to stabilize her.

"Why are you helping her?" Godwin asked in annoyance.

"Because she's my comrade."

"Huh? Even if it was indirect, she was trying to kill you."

"Yep, but she's still my comrade."

"I hate bad guys who don't realize they're evil, but I don't like this kinda saintly act, either."

I could only manage a wry smile at Godwin's anger.

"It's not that at all. I'm not saying she wasn't the enemy. She was. It's just…" I glanced down at my still-trembling hand. "Whether she was a foe or not, I don't want my sister to suffer the feeling of having killed someone she traveled with for so long."

Ares was our enemy. I didn't regret killing him. However, I wasn't able to simply discard him as some faceless opponent. We'd spent a lot of time together.

"If that's all, then okay, I guess…" Godwin looked a little bit ashamed and just dropped the matter.

"More importantly, we need to go help Ruti now," I said.

Everyone had downed a cure potion, and Rit had used her spirit magic to heal Mister Crawly Wawly since he couldn't drink one. Even so, it was evident that we were in pretty rough shape.

"Are you going to go, Red?" asked Rit.

"Of course," I replied.

"Then I'll go, too," Tisse stated as she stood up.

Mister Crawly Wawly was resting in Rit's hands, but when Tisse stood up, he raised his leg to indicate he would come as well.

"I'll be all right. You just focus on recovering, Mister Crawly Wawly," Tisse said to the spider.

"Sorry. If I could only focus my magic better...," Rit apologized.

"You've done more than enough considering all your injuries. Thank you for healing him."

Out of everyone, Rit had been hurt the worst. She had taken a direct hit from one of Ares's spells. There were still gruesome burns and cuts all over her body. The wound on her leg hadn't fully closed, either, forcing her to sit awkwardly on the ground.

"Taking out Shisandan will put an end to this. After that, we just need to find Danan and get out of here," I affirmed.

No sooner had I done so than a scream reverberated up from the hole in the floor. An intense crash accompanied the cry.

"Ruti?!" I exclaimed.

It was unmistakably my sister's voice, but she never shouted like that, even in battle.

I rushed over to the aperture, Thunderwaker in hand, ready to jump. However, a figure leaped nimbly up out of the hole before I had a chance and landed right in front of me.

"Ruti! I'm so glad you're safe."

It was indeed my little sister, but there was no expression on her face. One of the Holy Demon Slayers Shisandan had been wielding dangled loosely in her right hand.

"Ruti? Are you okay?" Something wasn't right. I started to approach her. "Huh?"

Suddenly, Tisse violently grabbed my shoulder, pulling me back and putting herself between Ruti and me. Then there was a terrible sound and a streak of blood.

"Tisse!!!"

Crimson dripped slowly from the Holy Demon Slayer. Tisse dropped to the ground. Thankfully, I managed to catch her, but a scarlet stain began to spread across her clothes before my eyes.

"No…Ms. Ruti…he's…your brother…don't…hurt him…"

Ruti had attacked Tisse. Her gaze remained fixed on us, face still utterly blank.

"Th-the murderous impulses from the medicine!" Godwin shouted.

He was referring to the Devil's Blessing's side effect. Memories of what had happened a while back in Zoltan flashed through my mind.

Could it really have affected Ruti?!

Swords met, and a metallic screech echoed through the hall.

"Rit! Godwin! Take care of Tisse!" I set the wounded girl down and put all my strength into my arms, locking swords with Ruti. Wasting no time, Godwin grabbed Tisse's limp body.

"Gh?!"

The moment I spared a glance away from her, Ruti kicked me in the stomach. My body howled in pain from the violent shock. Immediately, she followed it up with a slash that I caught with Thunderwaker.

My ears caught a distinct fracturing sound. I sprang backward several paces to get some distance from Ruti. Once I did, I looked down at Thunderwaker.

"…Thank you for everything…"

The weapon's blade was dotted with deep fractures. It was barely holding together after blocking Ruti's attack. Thunderwaker would probably never fight again. If it hadn't survived that slash for me, I would have been split in two. To the very end, that sword had been a true masterpiece.

I gently set Thunderwaker on the floor and placed my hand on the hilt of the bronze sword hanging at my waist. I assumed a stance, ready to face Ruti.

"A-are you crazy?! You really think you can fight with that shitty thing?!" Godwin shouted from behind me.

His outburst certainly wasn't without merit. A bronze sword was a cheap little thing not remotely comparable to Thunderwaker.

Ruti slowly raised her weapon. I focused every bit of myself on her. This was undoubtedly going to end quickly.

Bronze swords were weak, and their blades dull. That was because bronze was a more pliable material than steel. That malleability meant it would never be as strong as steel, but I had no other option.

Matching my timing to Ruti's strike, I drew the sword not from the hilt, but from beneath the cross guard, holding it by the blade.

This was called Bahamut-style cross-guard reversal. It was not a martial art granted by a blessing. Just an ordinary technique one had to practice to learn. A defensive maneuver where you drew the sword by the blade and used the guard and hilt to catch the opponent's cut. It was a technique that only worked with equipment like the steel longswords the Bahamut Knights used where the blade, grip, and guard were all forged as a single piece of steel. Thankfully, my bronze sword had similarly been cast in a single mold.

Typically, the reversal demanded you be wearing gauntlets. You were gripping an edge, after all. However, with a dull bronze sword, I wasn't going to lose any fingers doing it bare-handed.

Ruti's vertical slash sped down. This was a Holy Demon Slayer, a weapon that had already destroyed a renowned blade. A bronze sword couldn't hope to meet it on even terms. Fortunately, because of the extreme difference in hardness, the bronze sword didn't snap outright. Instead, the Holy Demon Slayer cut into it like a knife into butter, moving from the hilt down into the blade itself.

"!!!"

At that precise moment, I gripped tight and twisted with every bit of strength I had.

Ruti's weapon was embedded in the bronze sword, so when I rotated the bronze sword, the holy blade's momentum was added to the turn. The combined force of it all wrested the Holy Demon Slayer from Ruti's grip.

There was a clatter as both blades fell to the floor.

It was almost like using a wooden shield to steal an opponent's weapon, but this was the first time I'd ever done it with a sword. Thankfully, it actually worked!

While Ruti was without an armament, so was I, and she still had magic and boundless raw strength. My loss was guaranteed.

"..." Ruti stopped moving. She didn't rear back to unleash a deadly punch.

"I'm so glad we asked Godwin about Devil's Blessing before all this," I muttered.

Devil's Blessing's violent urges were brought about by the demon blessing it imbued. But the drug Ruti took was different. The blessing it manifested was one born from within Ruti. Thus, there was no reason for it to drive her to murder, since there was no way she would ever want to go around killing people. As her older brother, I was confident in that.

Since it wasn't the medicine, the source of her sudden outburst had to be elsewhere. By process of elimination, there was only one other source.

"Her other blessing. The Hero's blessing."

It was the blessing's last stand in the face of Ruti's determination to walk her own path. Perhaps Shisandan's strange swords had somehow spurred it on. The Hero had intended to kill any who had dared to allow Ruti to abandon her quest.

A single teardrop fell to the floor. I moved closer to Ruti and gently pulled her into a hug.

"Kh... Aaaaaaaaaaaaaaaaaaagggggghhhhhh!!!"

Words couldn't express how terrible being forced to attack her best friend, Tisse, and me had been for Ruti. She screamed in a swirl of rage, grief, regret, and relief, bawling as I held her in my arms.

*   *   *

There was a clank as the elevator's brakes engaged.

"Hn? Guess things really have resolved already."

Danan and Albert stepped out of the lift.

Huh? What's Albert doing here?

"Theodora!" Seeing the Crusader collapsed on the ground, Albert turned pale and sprinted over.

"She's okay. The wound is deep, but it's not life-threatening," I assured.

"…Thank God…"

Evidently, he had been with Theodora. There was a lot that needed clarifying, including things with Ares, but the time for that was later.

Danan seemed shocked to see the Hero crying.

"I owe you for earlier, Danan. Thank you," I said.

"I don't need your thanks. Sorry I was late," replied the burly man.

"And I don't need your apology… Shisandan is dead… Ares, too. It's all settled."

"I see."

Danan and I glanced over at the Ares's lifeless body. Neither of us was entirely pleased about the victory.

"Red! Ruti!" Rit suddenly cried. "I can't heal Tisse wounds with my magic! Hurry!"

Ruti immediately left my arms and rushed to Tisse without even bothering to wipe the tears from her face. Danan and I hurried after her.

"Tisse!"

The girl's face was pale, and she was unconscious. Her clothes were stained a deep-red shade.

"She's stopped breathing, and there's no pulse!" Rit was on the verge of tears, realizing that her magic and potions wouldn't be enough to save Tisse.

"Leave it to me," Ruti stated, holding out her right hand. The Hero's skill Healing Hands was capable of restoring someone's body even from the verge of death. It was an entirely different process from the typical Cure spell. It was an incomparable ability that rivaled the most powerful clerical arts, even at level 1. Not only that, but its effect also increased dramatically as the skill level grew. Even if Tisse was beyond the help that Rit could provide, Ruti would save her.

Unfortunately, nothing happened.

"Why?! ...I can't connect with my blessing!!!" she exclaimed.

"What? Did it temporarily stop responding after that rampage?!" I asked frantically. Then I recalled something I'd heard when I had spoken with the wild elves about their hidden medicines. Frequent use of substances that manipulated blessings could lead to blessings falling into slumber. This was how they referred to a temporary loss of power.

The cause was different, but the end result seemed the same— Ruti had temporarily lost access to the powers of the Hero.

"Why?! Why?! ...You're the one who was always dragging me around, pushing me into battles I never wanted to fight... You're the one who hurt Tisse...so why are you shutting up the only time I actually want your help?!" No matter how much Ruti tried to access the Hero's abilities, regardless of her tearful pleadings, the blessing did not respond.

"Ruti..." Tisse was dying before our very eyes, and there was nothing we could do.

Mister Crawly Wawly tilted his head as he tapped Tisse's hand with both his legs over and over, trying to wake her up. When she saw him, she didn't smile as she usually did.

"H-hey... You guys are all heroes, right? Isn't there anything you can do?!" Godwin shouted as he watched on.

Neither Danan nor I had any way to save Tisse now.

"Nooo! I finally...made a friend...and I...I...with my own hands!!!" Ruti wrapped Tisse in her arms and started crying.

There must be something…something I can do! If only my blessing hadn't been Guide! If I could just use magic!

"Let me see what I can do," called a voice from behind us. Theodora, supported by Albert, was staggering over.

"Theodora…," Ruti whispered.

"My role is to heal my comrades."

Danan and I stepped aside to let her through.

"C-can we really trust her?" Godwin asked nervously.

As far as he was concerned, the woman was an enemy who had appeared out of nowhere and pushed Rit and me to the edge of death, so his doubt was understandable.

"Yeah, it's okay," I replied. My faith in her had never wavered.

"Thank you for trusting me, Gideon." Theodora smiled weakly and had Albert lower her down next to Tisse and Ruti. "Regenerate."

The high-level clerical art spell enveloped Tisse's form in a warm glow. Her massive wound gradually closed, and the color returned to her face.

"Her pulse is back!" Rit was crying as she held Tisse's arm, her face filled with joy.

Ruti placed her cheek right next to Tisse's lips. "Her breathing, too," she managed hoarsely.

Tisse was saved!

"That should suffice." Having finished her work, Theodora exhaled deeply, losing strength and collapsing against Albert. "My apologies for setting such a pathetic example," she said to him.

"Don't worry about it. Now you should focus on tending to your own injuries! I used all of the cure potions on Danan. I don't have any left!"

Yet Theodora made no attempt to heal her own wounds. Instead, she looked listlessly at Ruti. "I won't ask you to forgive me. I still believe that I had no choice but to do what I did."

"…Even if that meant killing Big Brother?"

"It was for the sake of saving the world. You have no more intention of continuing as the Hero, right?"

"…"

"Of course not. Out of all of us, you alone were forced into the fight. No one has the right to judge you for finally living as you please."

"I never would have expected you to say that," Ruti admitted.

Theodora's voice was spiritless. She claimed she'd had no other choice, but her eyes betrayed regret.

"Why didn't you chase after Gideon when he left?" the Crusader asked Ruti.

"…"

"Because finding him was not important to the Hero's journey? That doesn't seem right to me. Our party crumbled without him. You had to have recognized that, too."

"Yes."

"So your blessing should have allowed you to chase after Gideon, then. His absence was disrupting the quest. Still, it didn't let you go to find him. For the longest time, I pondered why that was." A self-deprecating smile crossed Theodora's lips. "The answer was that Ares, Danan, me…even Gideon…not a single one of us was necessary to the Hero anymore. Even if our party dissolved, you could keep going alone, pushing ever forward without any need to sleep, eat, or drink. It was only kind mercy that kept you with us. Am I right?"

"…Yes," Ruti whispered softly.

So that was how it was. I had thought I was holding the party back, but from Ruti's perspective, every one of us was already nothing more than a burden.

"If you had continued, you would have reached a point where you were just pressing onward all alone, without ever stopping. Who would ever wish for such a life? Endless travel alone across the harsh lands of the dark continent would drive anyone into misery. But the Hero experiences no fear, no despair… As dull as I am, I realized one day just how lonely and cruel a fate it is to be you," said Theodora.

"Then, why?" Ruti pressed.

"Because you *had* to continue. Naturally, you questioned why it was your responsibility to safeguard a world that forced you into such a terrible role. However, I trusted that the Hero was the only one who could save everyone. I believed this world was something worth protecting, even if it meant sacrificing a young girl or dirtying my hands with the blood of her beloved brother. That is why Almighty Demis created the Divine Blessing of the Hero, and why I was born with the Divine Blessing of the Crusader. As a member of the clergy, that was my conclusion. Regardless of the erasure of your free will, I accepted that you had to live as the Hero."

"Theodora...but I..."

"I failed, though. God and the world will decide whether I was right or wrong, but I will not interfere any longer. I pray you have a free and happy life." With that, Theodora averted her eyes. "Thank you for everything, but this is enough. Please kill me. I betrayed you. I tried to murder someone precious to you, a man who was a precious friend to me. It is unforgivable."

Tisse stirred slightly in Ruti's arms. Seeing that, Theodora smiled ever so slightly.

"I'm glad I was at least able to save your friend... I was always a burden, but perhaps this means I managed to fulfill my duty, if only slightly."

Ruti looked at her, remaining silent.

"Please, wait!" Albert shouted. "I—I know this is probably not something someone as mediocre as I has any right to be saying! But please, forgive Ms. Theodora!"

"Albert...," I muttered.

The once-haughty and prideful man was now lowering his head for the sake of another. I never thought I'd see the day.

"I always dreamed of becoming a hero. The kind who could change the fate of the world. I dreamed of being like all of you. But I never understood how terrible that life could be. Ms. Theodora didn't know what to do. She was always struggling with it. Though it seemed she sided with a demon, she turned around and protected Mr. Danan. Her actions were inconsistent. But that's because Ms. Theodora couldn't reconcile Demis's teachings and her own feelings for her friends. She may have been mistaken, even foolish, but she was a true hero. She fought for the world as best she knew how. So please, I beg you, spare her life!" Head still lowered, Albert was pleading desperately with Ruti. It was something that only he, a man who'd wanted more than anyone to become a hero and failed, could say.

Ruti gave no reply, her gaze fixed on Albert for a few moments. After a bit, Tisse finally opened her eyes.

"Ms. Ruti…you're okay…"

"Tisse?!"

While not nearly fully recovered, the Assassin was looking much better. After some proper rest, she would be able to move again. Seeing her open her eyes, Mister Crawly Wawly joyously leaped onto her shoulder. Watching him dancing so happily brought a smile to Tisse's face.

"Yes, I'm sorry for troubling you," she managed.

"Please don't. Me worrying isn't something you need to apologize for… I'm glad you're safe now, and I'm sorry for hurting you." Ruti gently embraced Tisse, relieved.

I was glad, too, of course—we all were. Grinning, Rit took my hand.

Ruti faced Albert and Theodora with a soft expression. "It's okay. I can't forgive you for trying to hurt Big Brother or Rit, but it's because of you that Tisse is alive. So I can leave it be."

Ruti glanced over at Rit and me.

"Tisse is my friend, too. And besides, the only wounds I have are from Shisandan and Ares," I said.

"She's mine as well. She risked her life to protect me. I'm just glad she's okay," Rit added.

Ruti nodded. "No one holds a grudge against you, so I won't do anything, but…" She glanced down for a moment before continuing. Although her voice sounded apologetic, it carried a clear determination. "I am going to live my life as Ruti."

"I see," replied Theodora.

My little sister was silent for a moment, as if she was pondering the best way to express her feelings.

"I never once thought of myself as a hero. And I'd say that, if anything, you were the real hero. You're the one who struggled, fought, and bore so many wounds for the sake of the world."

"Me? That's absurd...," Theodora refuted.

"You're the one who tried to save the world. Even though you're wounded, you still agonize over what is right. I think perseverance is the true proof of the hero."

Having said her piece, Ruti passed the broken Holy Demon Slayer to Theodora. The woman stared at the blade, taking in Ruti's words, trying to wrap her head around it.

"Theodora, I think the real hero is meant to be lonely," I said.

"What do you mean?"

"I'm not talking about someone who just happens to have the right Divine Blessing, but a person who sets out to help because they chose to do so. They wouldn't be nearly as strong as the Hero, but they would draw a group of heroes to them who all sought to save the world. Working together, they could even defeat the demon lord in time. True heroes are those who fight for others because they want to, regardless of what a blessing commands."

Theodora sank into thought for a little bit. Gradually, her expression relaxed. Finally, she placed her hand to her own wound and healed herself with magic.

"Gideon... No, Red."

"What?"

"Do you think I can become a guide?"

"I don't have any inherent skills. So if you wanted to, I'm sure you could do it."

"I see... Searching out and instructing the kind of people you described sounds a lot better than turning my spear on my comrades for the sake of heavenly law." She glanced down at the broken Holy Demon Slayer, looking at the face reflected in the blade. What met her gaze was a woman at peace.

And with that, the battle in the ancient elf ruins drew to a close. Everyone rested there for a day, and the following morning, we made the trip back to Zoltan.

Chapter 6

After Happily Ever After

With the battle in the ancient elf ruins settled, we returned to Zoltan the next day.

"Ahhhhh." I yawned lazily out in front of the shop. "Ares, you asshole..."

Upon returning home, Rit and I discovered that our beloved little shop had been completely ransacked. I had been indignant, but Rit's rage was a sight to behold. Fortunately for Ares, he was already dead, so Rit turned her anger into motivation. Even though we had just returned from one of the worst fights of our lives, she had run all over Zoltan arranging the repairs.

"I'll put up the money for it, but we're getting this repaired immediately." I could tell from her expression that she wouldn't hear any dissent, so I just quietly nodded.

The plans had thankfully been settled quickly, and work was scheduled to start today. We had to close for the craftsmen, who'd be arriving soon. I was outside, cleaning up in anticipation of their arrival.

"Ah, snow."

Out of the corner of my eye, I noticed a white snowflake floating through the sky.

Sparse flurries drifted here and there, never reaching the earth, as the wind kept them afloat. While it never blanketed the ground, snow in southern regions had its own unique sort of charm.

"Big Brother."

Turning around, I saw Ruti wearing an alabaster dress and a matching white hat. She had picked out the outfit when I'd accompanied her on a trip to a nearby shop. There was no sword at her waist, no pieces of magic armor encasing her. She had already removed all of her rings, amulets, and other ensorcelled gear. Ruti was an average girl now.

However...

"*Achoo.*"

"It's cold out here."

Even in Zoltan, wearing a dress with no jacket in the snow was obviously going to be cold.

"Eh-heh-heh." Despite the sneeze, Ruti looked content. "I'm so happy. I can't remember how long it's been since I felt chilly."

"You'll get sick like that, you know," I chided.

"I've never been sick before. I can't wait."

I slipped my jacket off and put it over her shoulders.

"Here. My jacket will clash pretty horribly with your outfit, but take it anyway."

"...So warm..." Ruti sounded no different than any other young woman, and she smiled sweetly.

She hadn't lost the Hero's blessing. It was still there inside her, but that nameless one that had been born inside her had gained a name—New Truth. According to Ruti, in the strictest sense, it wasn't really a Divine Blessing. She apparently could not feel Demis's presence when she connected with it, something that every person felt when they reached out to their Divine Blessings. That meant God had not granted it. If the church found out, it would cause an uproar for sure. New Truth also possessed no impulses, which seemed to mean that it did not serve a role.

Other than those two points, however, it was fundamentally the same as any Divine Blessing. It had levels and skills, and defeating opponents with a blessing would allow it to grow. Ruti said the skills were very different, though. She couldn't freely pick and choose ones to learn upon leveling up. Instead, she had to fulfill specific requirements to unlock them.

Thus far, she had one skill, called Ruler. It was a pretty crazy ability that let her either nullify or forcibly activate the skills of anyone she touched. In a world where blessings determined the vast majority of combat abilities, such a power wasn't just unfair; it was basically cheating.

At this point, not even the mightiest demon lords of legend could lay a finger on Ruti. However, the best news of all was that she could use this skill on herself. Currently, Ruti was using that to control the Hero's blessing, nullifying almost all of her immunities.

"*Achoo.*"

"Red, Ruti, how long are you going to stay out in the cold?" Rit had come to check on us because we had been out for so long. "Oooh, such lovely, fluffy snow. But you're going to catch a cold."

"We should head indoors. You haven't had breakfast yet, right, Ruti? I'll go make something, so you just relax."

"I can't wait," she replied.

We hurried out of the cold, but Ruti and Rit turned around, reluctant to go inside just yet, wanting to watch the white snow dancing in the sky just a little longer.

*   *   *

After the battle in the ruins, Theodora had left Zoltan with Albert in tow. The pair had decided to travel areas beset by the demon lord's forces.

"This is farewell."

With that final good-bye, Theodora departed and never looked back. Ruti had tried to give her the armor and gear she had used on her journey, but Theodora refused.

"If the day ever comes when you decide you want to fight again, you may need it."

I was sure we'd never see Theodora in Zoltan again.

As for Danan, he would be staying at a local infirmary to focus on recovering for a half a year. He'd really pushed himself. The hot-headed Martial Artist was going to have to behave himself for a while.

We let Godwin go. Ruti no longer needed Devil's Blessing, and his efforts had been crucial to our victory over Ares. Ruti decided to turn a blind eye to his crimes as an expression of gratitude for everything he'd done. Had she still been the Hero, that would have been impossible for her. She gave Godwin a good amount of traveling money. He said he planned to make for the archipelago kingdom where the church had less control.

"Out there, I bet even a hunted heretic like me can get by," he stated, then he glanced at me and laughed. "Yeah, maybe I should try running an apothecary."

✳   ✳   ✳

"Today's breakfast is a bacon and white bean tomato soup, a little pizza with sauce using the leftover tomatoes, and fresh-squeezed orange juice."

"'Thanks for the meal!'"

Everyone said in unison to me.

"Your food is always so delicious," Ruti remarked with a spar-kling smile. She was really enjoying herself, as if all the joy that had been suppressed by the Hero blessing was finally being set free.

"Are you going out with Tisse later?" I inquired.

"Yeah."

The two were looking to buy a farm in northern Zoltan. Their plan was to grow medicinal herbs. Many were in high demand, but there was not much supply because raising such crops yielded little. That inefficiency of return kept most farmers from planting medicinal herbs, but Ruti wanted to try her hand at it.

"We're going to look for someone willing to sell us some land."

I never dreamed I would see the day when Ruti had an ambitious expression on her face. After being forced to be the Hero for so long, she was finally taking on a challenge that she had elected herself. As her brother, I couldn't be happier for her.

*   *   *

"Hey, Red!" Gonz called out as he entered the shop. "I know you're closed for the day, but Tanta caught a cold."

"So you need some medicine? Give me just a minute."

I pulled one week's worth of cold remedy from a pile of other drugs on the counter that had survived Ares's tantrum.

"Did things turn out okay with your little sister?" Gonz asked.

"Yeah, that's all taken care of now," I replied.

He looked relieved to hear that as I passed him the bag of medicine. "Good, you should give me a proper introduction sometime."

My failure to provide a suitable explanation last time must have worried him. Still, unlike everyone else living in Zoltan, Gonz didn't pry. He enjoyed his gossip, but he knew that certain lines shouldn't be crossed.

Regardless, I wanted to give Ruti the chance to meet everyone properly. The Hero part would have to be kept secret, but my friends deserved the chance to get to know her.

"Yeah, we can all go hang out together sometime."

And it wasn't just Ruti, either. I wanted folk to get acquainted with Tisse and Danan, too. They were true allies who had fought alongside me.

*   *   *

In the afternoon, Ruti, Tisse, Danan, and I gathered at the church at the center of Zoltan.

"Almighty Demis, we commend unto you your faithful child in this, his first and final pilgrimage to your side. The life he led is engraved in his Divine Blessing along with whatever sins he committed. We commend his blessing unto thee. If his Divine Blessing be filled with virtue, please guide him to nirvana. And be he not yet ready to pass through the gates, then please grant thine child Ares rest at thine side until such day as thou grant him a new Divine Blessing."

The priest sprinkled fragrant oil over Ares's face as he lay in the casket. The faint scent of snow—a universal symbol across all of the continent of Avalon—filled the air. It was a pleasant smell, but because it was a staple of funerals, snow rose oil was always associated with the image of death. As churches used it so regularly, each one had a bed of the flower, reinforcing the connection.

It was said that every bard in Avalon would compose a ballad to the snow rose at some point in their life. I didn't have any musical talent, but I couldn't deny that the imagery and fragrance stirred something in my heart.

The four of us, the priest, and his two aides were the only people in attendance. It was a simple send-off, but Ares did not have any complaints as he lay in the casket, eyes closed in silence.

According to doctrine, one's sins were recorded in their Divine Blessing, and those transgressions would be returned to Demis along with the Divine Blessing, leaving the person's soul free of wrongdoing, pure and ready to be reborn in their next life whenever they were granted a new Divine Blessing.

However, if the one in question forwent Demis's teachings in life, then God would not accept their blessing, and their sinful soul would suffer for eternity as a slave in the seven hells along with the demon overlords. That's what the church taught, anyway.

The priest rang a handbell. "Red," he instructed.

"Okay."

In accordance with custom, I placed a single piece of kindling into Ares's casket. Ruti, Tisse, and Danan followed in succession, each doing the same. The priest offered up one last prayer to convey to Demis how faithful Ares had been.

"The service is complete. I'm sure you are aware, but he will be cremated on the seventh day following his demise. You may visit then if you wish to meet him one last time…"

"…No, this is enough." I was a little bit unsure, but in the end, I declined. Ares was finally free from his struggles. It was all I could do to wish him a peaceful rest.

"Very well." The priest smiled gently and rang his handbell again. So it was that Ares the Sage's funeral came to a close.

Divine Blessings dwelled within all living creatures, but they did not exist in the dead. Ares was no longer at the mercy of the Sage.

While I didn't sympathize with the man, I still prayed his next life would be a more peaceful sort.

*   *   *

Twilight had already set in, and the sun cast red rays as it sank into the horizon.

"Haaah."

The last time I had borrowed a proper suit was for the party celebrating my shop's completion. Now I was wearing one to a comrade's funeral. Something about that left me feeling odd.

"Big Brother."

"What is it?"

"I'm sorry for having you bear so much."

I patted Ruti's head. "Thanks for worrying about me."

Killing Ares hadn't left me feeling remorseful. Still, I never wanted to kill one of my allies again.

"I guess I really am more suited to a slow life out here in Zoltan."

There was no weapon at my waist. I hadn't bothered to get a

replacement for my broken bronze sword. For some reason, I just couldn't bring myself to buy a new one until after Ares's funeral.

"Maybe I've changed a bit."

When I first settled in Zoltan, I'd avoided battle, but I still felt uncomfortable without a weapon. When Gonz had come to me for help curing Tanta's white-eye, I had strapped a blade on before leaving my house. Going with a bronze sword instead of a steel one had been my way of rebelling against the combat instincts I hadn't yet managed to shake.

"Shall we head back?" I asked.

Ruti took my arm with a smile. She didn't have a weapon at her hip, either. I grinned back, and the two of us strolled through Zoltan, looking for all the world like a pair of average, everyday siblings.

Making your way in this dangerous world unarmed was a difficult task. I planned to buy a new bronze sword tomorrow. However, that wasn't because of my blessing. Were I ever to draw it again, it would be because I wanted to protect those dear to me.

✳   ✳   ✳

"Looks like that's the last of it."

"Yeah."

Two days after Ares's funeral, Rit and I had finally gotten our shop cleaned up. Had we done all the work ourselves, it would have taken far longer, but thankfully, we'd received a lot of help. There were the craftsmen we'd hired, of course, but Ruti, Tisse, Gonz, Tanta, Mido, Nao, Dr. Newman, Stormthunder, Oparara, Al, Ademi, friends from the Adventurers Guild, and some off-duty guards had pitched in, too.

During the appreciation banquet Rit and I held for everyone, I introduced Ruti as my little sister, and we had a great time.

Truthfully, the last of the tidying was the cleanup after the cele-
bration, not Ares's rampage.

"Haaah." Rit sighed, frustrated. She'd been like that ever since
we discovered our shop had been ransacked. "If Ares were still
alive, I'd really let him have it for this," she muttered as she started
shadowboxing.

I chuckled and gave Rit tea I had made to help her relax. "Here,
drink some of this. We should get bed before too long."

"Yeah."

That was enough to get her to sit, at least. It looked like she was
finally settling down.

"...The bed...," Rit whispered as she stared down at the mug.

"Hn?"

"He destroyed our bed."

"Ah...yeah..."

It wasn't exactly unheard of for aristocratic ladies to hide letters
inside their sheets. Ares had been convinced that I was in secret
contact with Ruti for some nefarious purpose. He'd destroyed our
bed, searching for nonexistent evidence of conspiracy.

Obviously, even if I had been in contact with Ruti, there was no
way Rit or I would have hidden the messages in a place like that. It
just went to show how desperate Ares had been.

"That was our bed..." Rit's voice quivered as she lowered her gaze
to the cup in her hands.

"Rit..."

This upset her far more than I thought. Why?

I moved over next to her, and she leaned against my shoulder.

"Sometimes at night, when it's time to go to sleep, I get really,
really scared," Rit admitted in a listless sort of tone that felt very
unlike her.

"Scared?"

"I start wondering whether you will still be there when I wake up
in the morning."

"Don't be silly."

"But Danan…he understands just how amazing you are, too. It's not just me. Everyone needed your strength. You're the Guide. So long as you're there, everything is fine."

"My blessing isn't all that amazing. Other than starting out with a high level, it doesn't have anything special. No inherent skills, and the impulses are entirely minor. I can't even use magic or martial arts."

"No, I don't mean it in the sense of the blessing itself. The most important thing isn't the skills or the impulses. It's *you*." Rit looked me straight in the eyes. "You, Red the Guide, are amazing. The combination of the life you've led and your blessing have made you the type that everyone counts on."

"Maybe…"

My blessing existed to protect the Hero during the early steps of her journey. As such, it had urged me to keep the Hero safe. However, a blessing's power was proportionate to the strength of its impulses, and Guides' were incredibly weak. Not once in my life had I ever felt like I was being manipulated by my blessing. There was no way I had been meant to direct anyone other than Ruti.

Still, maybe Rit was right. I had been granted power in part to fulfill my role of guiding Ruti, and I had also put in a significant effort on my own to that same end. That experience put me in a position where I was qualified to support people other than my little sister. When I actually thought about it, that seemed obvious. However, in a world where Divine Blessings were the focus of most people's lives, Rit's view was an uncommon one.

"That's the Red I know. He's the one who showed me the way in Loggervia back when I was still really stubborn, everything I did failed, and I fell into despair. But I was conceited, thinking I was the only one who understood that side of you." Rit's eyes wavered as she looked me.

"That's why…when Danan came… Well, he was always so obsessed with defeating the demon lord… When I heard that he had halted his quest to search for you...I realized that everyone in the party must have understood how valuable you were. It made me glad, but I was also terrified. I wasn't the only one anymore. Part of me feared you wouldn't need me at your side."

"..."

"I understand that this life together is something you want, too. I really do get it. But I'm still so frightened that you might leave to guide someone else. I don't know how long I cried when you left in Loggervia. I managed to get through it then, but I don't know what I'll do if you leave now." Rit grabbed my hand with both of hers like she was clinging on for dear life. "This building...and that bed... they were ours. They held all the memories of us living together in Zoltan. So when they were all torn up like that...it was like you had lost your place to call home..."

"You're completely wrong!" Even I was surprised at how intense my response was, but I couldn't hold back. Seeing Rit freeze up in shock, I regretted the outburst, but I couldn't let her words go without explaining my feelings. "You've got it wrong, Rit."

"H-how so?"

I stood from my chair and kneeled in front of Rit. I was taller, so when I hugged her normally, my head was above hers. Down like this, however, I was gazing up at her face as she sat in her chair.

"R-Red?" She was confused as I wrapped my hand around her waist without saying anything. Then I hugged her, squeezing tight as I buried my head in her chest.

"I need you, Rit."

She was worried that I might leave because someone else needed me, but she had forgotten that it went the other way, too. I wanted her in my life just as much as she did me.

"This shop and our bed, the reason they became precious is because we shared them. You are the one I'm coming home to. If I hadn't met you here, I'm sure I would have given up my quiet life and taken Danan's offer. Without you, this wouldn't have been a home."

"Ah...ugh..."

"Do you remember when we first met again in Zoltan? We talked about things I wasn't aware of and blind spots I hadn't considered."

"Uh-huh. Of course. I'd never forget a conversation with you."

"Back then, do you recall saying that you realized I had my own weaknesses, but that was all the more reason you wanted to be together with me?"

"Yeah...I do...but..."

"That made me so happy. It was the first time anyone had ever told me that."

I was the Guide. My role was to assist the Hero as she began her journey. Like Rit pointed out, I could use my experiences to help out others, too. Yet the stronger the person I was guiding became, the less relevant I was. Plus, I would never be able to teach them martial arts or magic.

The reason I had ended my journey was not because Ares had deceived me. I had realized there was an insurmountable wall I would eventually reach no matter what I did.

"I'm only a Guide. Whomever I might instruct—at a certain point, they will overtake me and move beyond. There's no pupil I'd be able to stay with forever. In the end, everyone will go beyond my reach. That's my role."

If the Hero was a blessing destined to become so strong that everyone else was far behind, then Guide was one destined to see everyone disappear up ahead.

"Yet even after I had been kicked out of the party, when I was no longer the man who could lead the way for you anymore, even knowing all my faults...you still said you wanted to be with me. After struggling so desperately to keep pace with you all on our journey, I finally reached this slow and simple life—I finally reached you."

I squeezed Rit's body tightly so that she wouldn't disappear.

"...Red..."

"This is the end of my travels. Because I love you so, so much more than you realize."

"...!"

"That's why I'm not going to abandon you, no matter what might come. If anything, I'm scared of you leaving. When I realized Shisandan was alive, I wasn't scared of losing my quiet Zoltan days, I was petrified you would head off to fight him alone."

I could feel Rit's heart start beating faster as she hugged my head close.

"Will you stay with me forever, Red?"

"There's nothing I'd want more." At last, I had gotten out everything that had been lurking in my heart. "Please don't fret over me disappearing. I'll say it again: I love you, Rit."

"Yeah... I guess I've got nothing to worry about." Rit's body was trembling. I could hear her sobbing. "S-sorry...but I can't... I just can't stop crying..."

I don't know how long we stayed like that, but it was time well spent. Finally, though, Rit broke the silence.

"We're both so helpless alone. Just how weak have we gotten?" she asked.

"I'm not sure, but a life in Zoltan doesn't demand that kind of strength anyway," I replied.

"You're right."

It was okay to be weak. Perhaps that wasn't true in a world filled with monsters and demons, but for now, Rit and I were content that way. No one could convince me this feeling was wrong.

"...I want to go to bed..." Rit's whisper was so soft, I nearly missed it. Looking up, I saw her gazing down at me with scarlet cheeks.

"Y-yeah...I was thinking that, too..."

Rit's face turned even redder at my response.

*   *   *

Late that night.

Rit and I were sitting across from each other on the bed. Stormthunder had given us brand-new white sheets. We both fidgeted nervously, neither saying much, constantly looking at each other and then looking away again.

What are we doing? I thought, exasperated at our shared uncertainty.

Rit had changed into her pajamas and left the top three buttons undone. It should have revealed her cleavage, but she was clutching a pillow to conceal both that and how stupidly happy she was.

I'm not sure how to describe it, but at that point, even just her attempts to hide her embarrassment were unbearably adorable.

"Rit." I steeled myself and edged closer, until our knees were touching.

"Red." Rit inched nearer to me, too. Our legs slipped past each other, interlocking, and I could feel her warm thighs against mine. That alone made my face boil. I reached my hand out toward Rit.

"Umm, is it okay if I move the pillow?" I asked.

"Uh-uh…just undo it like this," she said.

"Wh-what…? I can't see my hands through the pillow."

"I'm sure you'll figure it out! And I'll be doing the same to you."

There was, seemingly, no other option.

The two of us started undoing each other's pajamas with a pillow sandwiched between us. Strange as it was, it shouldn't have been *that* difficult, but the softness of Rit's breasts proved distracting. I'd be lying if I said I wasn't getting excited. In fact, because I couldn't see, I was focusing much more on my sense of touch.

Her skin was like smooth silk. It felt so good that I could have kept stroking it forever. My finger accidentally moved down into her cleavage.

"Ahhh." A gentle moan crossed Rit's lips.

In that moment of surprise, the pillow slipped out of her arms and fell to the bed.

I could see the plunging V from her shoulders to just below her breasts. Rit's body really was gorgeous, captivatingly so.

Her face turned bright red, and her sky-blue eyes trembled. See-ing that, the love I felt for her welled up uncontrollably inside me. However, Rit struck before I could do anything.

"No fair! Revenge!" Rit squeezed her eyes shut as she slid her hands into my pajamas and started stroking my chest and stom-ach. A tremor of pleasure raced down my spine at first, but before long...

"Kh! Rit! That tickles! Ah-ha-ha-ha!"

The embarrassment must have been too much for her to take, because her eyes remained closed as she tickled my sides.

This woman could wield a large, difficult-to-handle blade like a shotel with unparalleled dexterity, and she was using every last bit of that deftness to tickle me mercilessly.

"Stop it, Rit! Ah-ha-ha!"

"Well?! Do you give up?!"

Give up? What? Perhaps she'd gotten so flustered, she'd forgotten what we were initially doing. *Wait. If the two of us are sticking our hands in each other's pajamas like this, at this rate...*

Snap.

"Uh..."

Amid my squirming, the last button on Rit's pajamas popped off. Her top slipped away, fully revealing her breasts. Rit's eyes went wide, and I couldn't look away.

"..."

"..."

The two of us froze. The only sound was the tick of the clock on the wall.

"Kyaaaa!" Snapping out of it, Rit leaned forward and clung to me.

That was certainly one way to hide her chest, but that soft, warm, pillowy feeling pressing against me was seriously testing the limits of my self-control.

"Did you see?"

"Isn't it a bit late to be asking that? ...You're beautiful."

"Argh!"

Rit's arms tightened around me. Her scent filled my nose, and I could feel my heart nearly bursting with love. Before I knew it, I was holding onto her as snug as she was to me.

"It's weird. Even this is so unbelievably satisfying," Rit said, her expression melting into happiness.

"True…just holding each other is amazing."

Rit looked up at me with her sky-blue eyes, and that gaze alone brought me more joy than any treasure I had ever found on my adventures.

"But." Rit kissed my neck. "It's not enough."

A thrill shot down my spine when I heard her coo that in my ear. The two of us slowly disengaged from our embrace. We got off the bed and stood facing each other. This time, we didn't try to hide behind a pillow as we quietly undressed.

Rit's last bit of clothing slipped to the floor. Moonlight from the window bathed her naked form in a pale glow.

"This is embarrassing…" Rit hugged her chest to cover her breasts. The pose was so unbelievably sexy that I couldn't help blushing. "You're practically beaming, Red."

Rit was hardly in a position to speak, though. She had the same silly grin.

"Umm… Uhhh… Yay!" Rit stood fretting for a moment before finally working up her courage and pouncing on me. I caught her in my arms and used my Acrobatics to slow the fall as we landed on the bed together.

Uwaaaaaaaaaaaaaaaah! We both screamed internally. I didn't have any skill that could read minds, but I was confident Rit had the same reaction I did.

We tended to spend a lot of time clinging to each other. While we still enjoyed that, it wasn't the sort of thing that got either of us worked up anymore. However, with nothing between our skin, it was a completely new experience.

Rit's body was so perfectly smooth and felt so good that I thought

I could get addicted to the feeling. There was just the faintest trace of sweat, and she was taut and supple with just the right amount of muscle. Her legs were long and slender, but her thighs had a voluptuousness, and the way they seemed to cling to me with our legs wrapped together was amazing.

With her breasts pressed against me, there was no doubt about how soft they were. There was a pleasant scent coming from her blond hair. Her slightly ragged breathing tickled my ear. The line from her bottom up her back was a gorgeous curve. Along that path was a faded scar, likely an old wound from an arrow.

Spend enough time adventuring, and you were bound to get injured at some point. Magic could close most wounds, but occasionally, blemishes remained.

Rit trembled when I reached down and gently caressed the ancient injury. To me, even her scars were endearing.

I let myself drown in the sensation of Rit's body on mine. My heart was already always on the verge of overflowing, and the joy just kept welling up.

"Reeedddd."

"Rit!" Her calling my name was enough to make my heart tremble. "I love you so very much. I love you so much, I can't even begin to explain how much I love you."

Argh, I don't even know what I'm trying to say anymore.

I could feel myself becoming more and more helpless. Rit's face drew closer, her eyes glistening, overcome with emotion. Our lips touched, and the taste of Rit filled my mouth.

It was undoubtedly a long kiss, but I couldn't judge for sure. During my days as a knight, I had honed my internal sense of time to keep it together during charges and surprise attacks, but that was all out the window now. Nothing mattered but Rit and me in this moment together.

"Sorry, Rit…I'm reaching my limit… I don't think I can hold back anymore."

"…It's the same for me, obviously…"

Sparks flew in my mind when I heard her passionate voice.

This time, I kissed her and started touching her body. When our lips parted, Rit was red to the tips of her ears, but smiling.

"I love you, Red."

Her whisper finally burst the dam holding my emotions in.

After that, there was no need for words.

∗   ∗   ∗

Rit was lying in my arms. We were both exhausted. I was too content to move again any time soon, and it looked like Rit felt the same.

Occasionally, we'd glance at each other, giggle, lean our heads together, and lightly kiss.

"I'm so happy…" Rit rested her head on my chest. "Living together with you, I was always so glad… I thought there couldn't be anything better, but…" She touched her stomach gently and blushed. "It's almost like you're still there… I'm so happy."

"Things only get better from here," I replied.

"Really?"

"Of course. I said this was the end of my journey before, but it's also the start of a whole new one."

"What kind?"

"One that's quiet, peaceful, and filled with wonder." I closed my eyes, imagining it as I put it into words. "The two of us working together in the shop, taking holidays together, having picnics out in fields of spring flowers, standing out in the winter snow in each other's arms again. Eventually, we may even start a family. Whether it's a boy or a girl, I'm sure things will be lovely. After a time, it'll just be the two of us again. By then, the tranquility might feel a little lonely. The shop will have aged. We'll need to start oiling the creaking doors before opening in the morning. At some point, I'll turn

into a little old man, and you'll turn into a little old lady. Should we have grandkids, we can help look after them. That might get us fretting about things getting boisterous again, but that sounds fun in its own sort of way..."

"That sounds like such a lovely journey..."

"It sure does. Let's walk that path together all the way to the end. And whenever we reach the conclusion of our adventure, we will both look back and say, 'What a marvelous trip.'"

Rit sat up, looking at me with her sky-blue eyes.

"Hey, Rit."

"What, Red?"

Basking in the beauty of her visage, I replied, "I asked you before, but what kind of gem do you like?"

Rit lay on top of me, arms wrapped around my neck. "Whatever you choose for me! The stone you pick will be my favorite of them all!"

"Okay."

"I'm so excited! I can't wait!"

"I can't get anything rare like back when I was adventuring, though."

"Scarcity has nothing to do with it. What it's worth and what other people think don't matter to me at all." Rit grinned from her perch on top of me, her pearly-white teeth gleaming. "It's the gem that will join us together. That makes it far more precious than any legendary item."

Rit kissed me again. As it continued, my heart started aching again. Before I knew it, I had wrapped Rit in a tight embrace again.

*   *   *

It rained the next day.

"A ring, huh...?"

I had made a mental list of all of the gems I knew and was leafing through each to figure out which was best suited for Rit. There wasn't a high demand for precious stones in Zoltan. In Central, you could find everything from irregular pearls to diamonds, from the cheapest baubles to the most expensive jewels. But not in Zoltan. Gems were only available when seafaring traders brought them, so stock varied depending on when you checked, and there was never a wide selection.

"I might have to reach out to one of the aristocrats, but I don't even know who to start with."

My budget was hardly large enough to haggle with nobles anyway.

"Guess that means the mountains."

If I ventured out to the Wall at the End of the World, there was supposedly a village of gem giants that were experts in jewels. Zoogs lived around the base of the range. Hopefully, they'd give me some directions.

"The night of the winter-solstice festival would be a good time."

It was as classic a time to propose as you could get. All that was left was to find a gem and get the ring made.

"Hey, Red, what are you smiling about?" Gonz asked, grinning suggestively.

He had come into the shop to escape from the rain.

"Nothing," I responded, just brushing it off.

Rit would be back in an hour. I couldn't help but smirk at that thought.

*   *   *

It had already been a week since Ruti had settled here in Zoltan.

"Thank you for your purchase," I said as I passed the medicine over to the customer.

Beneath the counter, the brand-new bronze sword I had gotten to replace my old one was sitting in its scabbard. Mogrim had given me a hard time about getting another bronze sword, but I had grown attached to the weak armament. The cheap, old weapon was like a symbol of my determination to live a quiet life.

"I've finished up the deliveries."

Shortly after the customer departed, Rit returned. She put away the empty medicine box and then sat down next to me. No sooner had she done so than I heard footfalls coming from out back.

"Big Brother, we've finished tending to the herbs in the garden."

It was Ruti and Tisse.

Starting today, I would be teaching them how to raise medicinal herbs in preparation for the farm Ruti wanted to build. For their first lesson, I had them prune a plant called redegg. It was a shrub that generally stayed under a meter tall and got its name from its crimson berries. During winter, it shed its leaves and went dormant. During that period, you needed to trim the branches to help concentrate the nutrients. Generally, you could prune around two-thirds and it would still be fine. Redegg was picked in the early days of summer, so with Zoltan's warm climate, that meant they were gathered pretty early.

While used in medicine, the plant had an eggplant-like flavor, so it was occasionally used in high-class cuisine. It was effective against dangerous illness like goblin fever. Demand for redegg was high, but its berries were small in the wild. Figuring out how to grow larger ones seemed like both a fun and useful puzzle to solve.

"Thanks. I'll check how you did in a bit, so feel free to relax for a moment."

"…I'll help, too," Ruti stated and then plunked herself down next to me, on the opposite side from Rit.

"Are you sure? I imagine it was hard work, right?" I questioned.

"Sitting down when your legs are tired feels really nice," Ruti responded with a sparkling smile.

And then she wrapped her arms around my left one and leaned against me.

"Grr!" In response, Rit grabbed my right arm. Something large and soft pressed against that arm—very different from Ruti's side.

"Nrgh." Ruti seemed vexed as she fixed Rit with a pointed glare. Rit wasn't backing down, however, firing back with a placid stare of her own. For a moment, the air became tense and strained. However...

"Gha-ha-ha-ha-ha!"

Both Ruti and Rit burst out laughing at the same time.

"What are you two doing?" I asked with a chuckle.

However, my eyes narrowed as I saw the tranquil aura around Ruti. The figure of the Hero that even Rit had once called scary was nowhere to be seen. All that remained was the young woman, Ruti.

"How exactly do I break up this sort of situation?" Tisse was watching the three of us, half-exasperated at our silliness and half-delighted at how happy Ruti looked. Mister Crawly Wawly tapped her shoulder, glad for the change in my sister, too.

Clang!

The bell on the front door rang loudly.

"M-Ms. Ruhr!" Megria from the Adventurers Guild burst into the shop. "An urgent request has come in! A band of ogres has come down from the Wall at the End of the World, and they're occupying a nearby village! The C-rank adventurers who went to take care of it got captured as well!"

Ruti released my arm and stood up. "Okay," she said with a nod.

At that, I reached beneath the counter, picked up Ruti's sword from its spot leaning next to mine, and handed it to her. It was the goblin blade filled with holes.

"I'll be back soon, Big Brother."

"Okay. Be careful."

Zoltan's lone B-rank adventurer, Bui, had disappeared. Ruti and Tisse had formed a party to fill the gap his absence created. It was only a part-time job, though.

The authorities in Zoltan had sounded Ruti out about taking the job, and even though she had insisted on the clause that it would only be in her spare time while farming medicinal herbs, they had officially promoted her to a B-rank adventurer. The name she had given for her paperwork was Ruti Ruhr. Unlike me, she didn't take well to an alias, so she settled on having the people close to her call her Ruti while everyone else used Ruhr.

Ruti slipped an armored coat with iron bits woven into it over her regular clothes. One could hardly call it sufficient protection for combat, but she had decided to commit to a style that wasn't all about battle.

My sister wasn't the Hero anymore, nor did she feel compelled to aid others. Still, that didn't mean she'd become the type to abandon those who were suffering and in need.

At first, she was a little bit hesitant about aiding people, but when I told her, "You finally got your freedom, so just do what you want to do without worrying about being captive to your blessing," it was like a weight had been lifted. She elected to become an adventurer who would help when she wished and wouldn't be pressured otherwise.

"I think Ms. Ruti truly is a hero. She fights because she believes in what she's doing, not because her blessing commands her," Tisse stated.

"You might be right." I nodded.

This was the path Ruti had chosen. Unburdened by her blessing, she was living a slow, heroic life. The gallant figure she cut as she walked away was hers alone. After so long, my sister was walking the path she wanted.

"Ruti! Is there anything you want me to make for when you get back?"

Hearing my voice, she turned toward me. "Honey milk, please," my little sister answered with a completely natural and utterly adorable smile.

The Hero had been saved, and everyone lived happily ever after.

Yet this wasn't the end of Ruti's story. The simple life that she had sought for so long was just getting started.

The Hero's Slow Life

Opening my eyes, I saw my little sister's cute face peering at me.

"Good morning, Big Brother."

"Good morning."

I wasn't surprised. This had been common during our travels together. Back then, Ruti would sometimes stare at my face all night because she had nothing to do. I had suggested reading a book every once in a while, but Ruti declined, saying it didn't feel right to force herself to read even if she didn't want to just because she had extra time. Thus, I had fallen into the habit of allowing Ruti to do whatever she pleased provided it didn't wake me up.

Picturing Ruti sitting beside me in a dark tent, leaning over to look at my face all night… It was just, well…

It was so adorable!

I mean, she was gazing straight at my face, right? Knowing that she thought I was so dependable lit a fire in my heart. Plus, it was reassuring to have her beside me all night. My dreams had always been pleasant with her there.

When I mentioned that to Tisse and Mister Crawly Wawly, though, they were taken aback. For the following two hours, Tisse walked around as awkwardly as a poorly crafted golem.

"Big Brother," Ruti called again.

"Ah, sorry. Guess I'm still a little sleepy. I'll get up now."

My sister nimbly pulled back as I sat up.

"Did you turn your Immunity to Sleep back on last night?" I asked.

"Yeah. I wanted to watch you. It's been a long time since I had the chance."

Gazing out the window, I could see a glum portrait of winter in Zoltan. Just how early was it?

Rit had gone to a nearby village yesterday to stock up on some herbs. She was staying the night and would be back in the evening. Ordinarily, I'd be the one to go, but...

"Thank you for keeping your promise, Big Brother," Ruti said happily.

I had told Ruti I'd show her around the harbor district today.

There was a rare herb—actually, it was a plant-type monster— called snake-eater grass that could be used as a substitute for blood needles in a few medicines. As luck would have it, a breeding ground of sorts for the creature had been discovered yesterday. The snake-eater grass had already caused a few problems, so a request was bound to show up in the Adventurers Guild soon. Whoever took the job would likely burn it all. That was the fastest way to get rid of it.

I wanted to defeat the monster and bring it back here before that happened, but I already had plans with Ruti. While I fretted over what to do, Rit had offered to go deal with the snake-eater grass herself.

"So shall we dine out for breakfast today?" I proposed.

"Your cooking is my favorite...but I'm interested to see what sorts of food there are in Zoltan, too," Ruti responded.

I couldn't help but smile at that. Not too long ago, the idea that Ruti would express interest in anything had been absurd.

I gently patted her hair, and she tilted her head a bit in surprise, but then her eyes narrowed like a contented cat's.

*   *   *

Zoltan's port was connected to the river.

Unfortunately, no one knew the waterway's name, though it likely had some kind of moniker back during the age of the wood elves. A particularly old half-elf claimed he was pretty sure it was something that started with "Mi" back in his grandparents' generation. However, every account like this differed. Supposed name meanings included river lit by the rising sun, dark of night river, summer's gleam river, and tranquil winter river.

This variety was due to wood elf culture. They believed that all things were in a state of continuous change. Thus, even a river became something else entirely to them depending on the seasons and years.

Meanwhile, to the humans who had settled here and created Zoltan, it was just "the river." They valued the waterway, of course, but a name was just a means of identifying something. So long as it was clear what you were referring to, that was enough for these lazy folk.

Wood elves went extinct long ago, but I would have liked to be able to sit down and talk with them just once.

They may have disappeared, but the river was still here, and we humans wouldn't be able to survive in this region without it, either.

"It's why we can enjoy this baked pike."

Shops in the harbor district catered to dockworkers and sailors, so you could find fish soup just about anywhere you checked. The establishment Ruti and I had stopped in was also an inn where ships' captains and officers regularly stayed, so it served proper breakfasts, too.

The pike had been steamed in fish stock, which really brought out the refreshing flavor of river fish. Its accompanying onion marinade was fantastic. The meal came with soft, white bread and some wine, despite it being morning.

"Delicious." Ruti seemed to be enjoying herself as she had her breakfast.

I'm glad it suits her tastes.

"Since we're in the harbor district…I guess we should check out the import market. After that, we can rent a sightseeing boat," I said.

"A sightseeing boat?"

"Yeah, you can pay to use one for a bit. We can ride it up the river and take in the sights."

"Just the two of us, on a boat…" Ruti glanced down. Her lips spread just a little, and I caught a tiny, restrained giggle. Then she looked back up, eyes gleaming. "That would be great."

✳   ✳   ✳

The market was packed and lively whenever a ship came in, but today it was almost entirely deserted—just a traveling merchant on a rowboat who had come back from the villages upriver.

"Hey there, apothecary!"

Someone called out to me as Ruti and I walked. The voice belonged to a shady-looking man named Pasquale. He lived here in the harbor district. Primarily, he worked as a counterfeiter, but he also served as a ship's navigator on the side. He had all sorts of scars on his lower legs, but it was the unspoken rule of Zoltan not to snoop into people's pasts. I didn't have any solid urge to pry, either.

"What's this? Fooling around with another girl? You've already got Rit, don't you?"

"This is my sister, Ruti Ruhr," I replied.

"Huh, never woulda guessed you had a sister. She's a real cutie, too," remarked Pasquale.

"Incidentally, she's the new B-rank adventurer, so if you try anything funny, you can count yourself lucky if you only end up half-dead," I responded.

"Seriously? Rit's one thing, but your sister, too? Do you have some kinda blessing that creates heroes?"

I couldn't help a wry chuckle at that. He wasn't entirely off the mark.

"As if a blessing like that could exist. So what'd you want?"

"I mean, I was sure you were on a date, is all. Look, these'd make a perfect present for her, right?" Pasquale was gesturing at the various jeweled earrings and tiaras lined up in front of him.

"They're all just fakes. Glass, right?" I pressed.

If he were selling authentic accessories, then I could add him to the list as a candidate for Rit's ring.

"I mean, yeah, obviously. But they're still pretty, ain't they? They're all masterpieces that I put my heart into polishin'," admitted Pasquale.

"So you say. No doubt you'll sell them at a markup since they're all such masterpieces, right?"

"I don't do that for people who know the grift. I'll sell 'em to ya for a fair price, accountin' for materials and labor."

"Hmmm."

I glanced over at Ruti.

Simply put, my sister was filthy stinking rich. She had found all sorts of legendary treasures during her travels and sold off supplies and loot taken from the demon lord's forces. The prizes she had were all so valuable that given the scale of the economy out here, there wasn't anyone who could afford to buy them. She had more wealth than the entire national budget of Zoltan. I'm sure she had payril silvers, too, though I had no clue how many.

Given that, buying her a glass bauble as a present seemed almost like an insult.

Ruti wasn't wearing any of it now, but she had a wealth of magical accessories, from mithril earrings to a buckle made from a scarce meteoric metal called redsky.

"Big Brother..."

"Hn? Did you want something?"

"Uh-huh... It can be the cheapest one; I don't mind."

I see...

"Okay, then I'll get you whichever one would look best on you."

"Yay, a present."

Ruti looked pleased, and she blushed bashfully.

With that, Pasquale and I descended into a sparring match. He tried to sell off the most expensive thing he could, but eventually, I put down the money for a particularly well-made pair of earrings and gave them to Ruti.

✳   ✳   ✳

We were riding a little yacht with one mast and a triangular sail. It was small enough that on a tranquil day, it only took one person to row. It wasn't equipped to carry payloads and didn't travel fast, but it was a river sightseeing boat, so that was more than enough.

"This should be about right." I maneuvered it so that just a little bit of wind would catch the sail. The boat lazily glided upriver. "All right, let's have lunch."

I had picked up some food at a stall before we left. Inside the paper bag was fried whitefish and sweet potato. Ruti and I dug in.

"In the northern district, there's a place with this foreign food called *takoyaki* that's really good, but it's a bit far from here," I said.

"I want to eat that with you next time," Ruti answered immediately.

"Got it. On our next holiday, we'll take a look around the northern district."

"Okay."

As the boat sailed gently upriver, Ruti and I watched as the townscape slowly passed by.

"This is so nice," Ruti stated. "I never thought I would get to spend a day like this with just the two of us again. I didn't think I'd have friends like Tisse, Mister Crawly Wawly, or Rit, either." She turned to look straight at me. "Thank you, Big Brother. Can we stay together like this forever?"

She had asked that once before, and I had dodged the question because I'd been about to join the Bahamut Knights at the time. Things were very different now, though. My goal these days was to live a simple, peaceful life.

"Yeah. I'll be by your side for as long as you want me there."

Hearing that, Ruti smiled as her eyes trembled, and she clenched her fist and did a little fist pump.

"Yay!"

*   *   *

Two days later, Rit, Ruti, and I went out to the mountain.

This time, it wasn't to fight. Our trip was only to gather some herbs. When Ares had wrecked the shop, a large portion of the plants in storage had gone bad. Tisse and Mister Crawly Wawly had stayed behind to watch the store for us.

"This is a white berry. I'm sure you know it's the base for magic potions, but have you ever seen the raw fruit before?" I inquired.

"No," answered Ruti.

I was also using the opportunity to teach my sister all I could about medicinal herbs, since she planned to start a farm for them. Given her current level, there was no way she would be able to level up her blessing out here in Zoltan. So it would be difficult for her to allocate skill points into Survival, the skill that allowed you to discern medicinal herbs from other plants easily. Thus, I was teaching her the distinguishing characteristics so she could tell for herself without using a skill. Using a skill guaranteed accuracy, but it didn't confer the actual knowledge. Learned information was more versatile.

"This is a fruit that looks very similar to white berries. It's called a gray berry. The name's a bit misleading, however. If you put it next to a white berry, it appears nearly identical. Can you see the difference?"

"Yeah."

"The Survival skill will tell you that this is just a weed that doesn't have any value and that it isn't a white berry, but it can still be used to make an ointment that's good for dealing with bug bites."

"Really?"

"Remember back when we were traveling, there was a salve we put on our arms and legs and neck when we were going through forests and marshes?"

"Oh, so that's what that was. You really are amazing, Big Brother."

Insect bites wouldn't trouble the nearly invincible Ruti, but this wasn't knowledge for the Hero anyway. It was just some simple stuff to help a young woman live her life.

Ruti wore a serious expression, but she seemed to be enjoying herself, listening intently.

"She just like you, Red," Rit said.

"Huh?"

Behind us, Rit had set down her basket filled with herbs. Seeing my surprise, she elaborated, "When you're preparing medicine and stuff, you have that same sort of focused look, but it's clear you're having fun... It's a lovely expression. You two really are siblings."

"Mph."

I held my hand up to cover my mouth. Seeing that, Rit tugged her bandana up to cover a giggle.

"Big Brother, you do the same sort of thing Rit does when you smile," Ruti remarked, looking just a little bit disgruntled.

Rit's eyes went wide, and then her cheeks flushed as she tried to conceal more and more of her face behind the bandana.

"Mph."

Ruti peered over at my smiling face and used her hands to try to pull her mouth into a smile. Trying to match my grin, I guess.

We stopped working for a little while, just smiling and laughing as we looked at each other. After that, we split up into two groups and spent about four hours gathering herbs.

"There we go."

Rit and I had finished harvesting polyp mushrooms that grew around a shady little creek that ran through the valley, and we'd just gotten back to where we had split up.

"Ruti?"

My sister had filled her basket full of white berries and was leaning against a tree trunk in the sunlight, eyes closed. She'd dozed off.

"That's a first."

Ruti was napping defenselessly. I guess she had gotten a little sleepy waiting for us with the unseasonably warm sunlight shining down.

To the Hero, napping was pointless, but for Ruti, that moment of peace wasn't useless at all. It was precisely the kind of thing I had always wanted her to experience.

"The weather really is nice," Rit said as she sat down at the base of a nearby tree.

"Yeah, it sure is."

I sat down and looked up at the blue sky. It was past three in the afternoon already. A thrush sitting on a tree branch glanced over at me and chirped. Returning the look, I held a finger to my lips.

"My sister is resting now."

However, the bird just cocked its head and flew down, trilling again right in front of us. I couldn't help chuckling when it puffed out its chest, as if bragging about how great its singing voice was.

Peaceful. It was such a lovely moment…

I started to doze off, but I opened one eye when I sensed something approaching. An owlbear was peeking out of the undergrowth. It was small; still a child. It was peering over at me as if looking for permission, so I signaled with a glance for it not to mind us. At that, the owlbear quietly wound its way behind Ruti. It was pretty considerate for a monster.

After going down the mountain a little ways behind Ruti, it picked up the corpse of a five-meter-tall mountain giant in its mouth and dragged it off into the distance. The giant must have attacked Ruti while she was gathering by herself. It had probably wandered down from the Wall at the End of the World.

"So peaceful."

While the owlbear disappeared into the distance, I closed my eyes again.

∗   ∗   ∗

The next day proved similarly tranquil, but dinner was a noisy affair because Danan came over to eat.

He had been so severely wounded and covered with bandages that for a while, it had looked painful just to sit up. Now he had recovered enough to walk around on his own. That was Danan for you.

After treating Ruti, Tisse, and Danan to an evening meal, I asked Rit to take care of the dishes and went out by myself to look at the night sky.

"Yo," a voice called out from behind me. It was Danan. "That was some great food. Your cooking really is the best."

"Thanks."

"It's a shame I won't get to enjoy it anymore once I start traveling again."

"So you really are going to head out once you're all better?" I asked.

"Yeah. I swore I wouldn't forgive the demon lord for destroying my home."

"I see."

He'd still be recuperating for a while yet, but he'd be gone in half a year at most. Danan was still a Martial Artist, even if my fight was over. Our paths had split.

"Hey, Red, I'm not the brightest guy, so I can't say I really understand it all, but…the thing this time…how do I put it…it feels like there were too many weird coincidences. You know what I mean, yeah?"

"...I do. For starters, why was Shisandan still alive? How did he know the Sacred Avengers were there? And why was he after them?"

I had heard from Theodora that the swords the Asura demon had wielded were relics from the first Hero. Like Danan, she had also suspected something strange was afoot.

However, the most suspicious part of it all was...

"Why were there five swords?"

"Right?"

The Sacred Avengers were long—about a meter. And it went without saying, but humans and elves only had two arms. Even dual-wielding, you would only need two swords. So why had there been five of them?

"It's too conspicuous to merely be a few spares...," I said.

"I can't imagine God being that generous," Danan concurred.

They were legendary weapons presented by God to the first Hero. Similar legendary armaments and armor existed, but in every instance, they were always unique objects. I'd never heard of extras.

"From what Ruti heard Shisandan say, it seems like..." I trailed off. It wasn't that there were three or four extras; it was that one had been missing. The second-generation Hero had taken one, leaving five behind. "There were originally six of them. That would be my guess. Then the numbers add up."

∗   ∗   ∗

Somewhere on the dark continent in the subterranean realm of Underdeep, inside the demon lord's castle that served as the capital of the Asura demon nation known as Asura Kshetra sat a towering shadow upon a throne.

The gigantic figure stood more than five meters tall. His body and six arms were sculpted like one would have imagined the ideal warrior. His expression was the embodiment of rage. In the middle of his forehead was a third eye filled with flames, opened wide.

Taraxon, the Raging Demon Lord. The ruler of the forces invading the continent of Avalon and a great Asura demon warrior. Taraxon had destroyed the tribe of wrath demons that were true heirs to the throne.

Four of Taraxon's arms moved as if searching for something, while the other two remained still. From the motion, a seal formed before his chest. Before long, light started to emanate from the ground before him. The glow increased, expanding into a massive, luminous ball before taking shape and gaining size. Finally, it transformed into the figure of the Asura demon Shisandan.

Shisandan knelt before Taraxon and lowered his head in a practiced manner.

The demon lord's four moving arms stopped, and Taraxon looked down at the kneeling Asura as he spoke.

"Hail, hero. Your death was unfortunate."

Asuras, having not been created by Demis, were far removed from the traditional cycle of life and death. Their souls returned to the Asura lord to be reborn again. Asuras were not originally a powerful race. In the age when New Truth was everywhere, Asura heroes were defeated and slain countless times.

However, they learned from their losses, understanding more with each cycle. Despite so many deaths, they had persisted without losing hope and continued to fight until they'd finally destroyed the one who ruled New Truth.

That unbreakable resolve, that way of life, that was what it truly meant to be a hero in the teaching of Asura philosophy.

"Take some time to regain the strength you've lost, proud Shisandan."

"Sir!" Shisandan nodded emphatically.

Even for Asuras, death meant losing both magical power and physical strength. Yet it also conferred the courage to attain something even greater. This was why no Asura feared death nor defeat.

I must train myself even further.

Shisandan thought back to Ruti's single blow, in awe of the destructive power that she possessed.

Would he ever really be able to match that might?

The road was undoubtedly long, perhaps even endless. But for an undying Asura, there was nothing more gratifying.

Shisandan's lips spread into a warped smile as he knelt there, head bowed.

✻   ✻   ✻

To the west of Zoltan, on the highway just past the border, Godwin sat on a grassy knoll beside the road, making a stew.

"Today's lunch is a brew of beef jerky and pickles, huh?"

The only seasoning he had was salt.

It had been a long time since Godwin had cooked out on the road, and it honestly did not look particularly appealing.

"Haaah. It wasn't that long ago I was Bighawk's right-hand man and was livin' the good life…" Lifting a spoonful to his lips, he could not taste anything other than salt. Godwin sighed. "Even if I'm headin' for the archipelago kingdom, I'm gonna hafta find a merchant ship or caravan first. I should see about getting hired as a guard, so I can take it easy while makin' some money and gettin' food for free."

Suddenly, Godwin heard the sounds of travelers approaching from the distance. The man was an escaped convict. He was out of Zoltan, but there might still be someone who recognized him.

After dousing his fire, he grabbed the pot and put a lid on it, then he crouched down to hide in the meadow.

A merchant procession of three horse-drawn carts drew close. The broker holding the reins was someone Godwin recognized from Zoltan.

This is getting dangerous…

Smoke from his fire still rose into the air, and the smell of the soup he had been making remained detectable.

Godwin cursed himself for believing he wouldn't run into anyone on their way to Zoltan.

His face turned pale. This particular merchant had a good reason to hold a grudge against him. It had been a long time ago, but back when Godwin was a grunt with the Thieves Guild, he had been ordered to interfere with that dealer's sales.

I'm sure he's got it out for me. He'll definitely recognize me... Godwin was getting nervous when he suddenly remembered the little vial in his bag. *Oh yeah, I have that invisibility potion Rit gave me.*

Whether Rit had forgotten about it in all the commotion or she didn't care about losing it, Godwin had held onto it.

Wasting no time, he downed the contents of the vial in a single gulp. He, his clothes, and his luggage all vanished.

There, now it should be fine.

Godwin breathed a sigh of relief before remembering that the potion did not mute sounds and covering his mouth with both hands.

The little caravan was getting nearer.

Godwin, now invisible, was lying beneath a rise in the ground. There were two warriors on horseback guarding the traveling merchants. Seeing the remnants of the fire, they looked around from atop their mounts, but didn't spot anything that gave them further pause. The merchant driving the carts looked a little bit nervous as he passed right in front of Godwin.

Yes!

Unfortunately, the victory was short-lived. The grass before him trembled.

"Huh?"

The verdant blades twisted like a living creature, wrapping around Godwin and pinning him down.

Wh-what the hell's goin' on?!

He panicked, and the guards protecting the procession looked surprised. One of the coaches stopped, and a single high elf woman stepped out. Her eyes looked straight at Godwin even though he should have been undetectable.

"Plants do not see with eyes the way we do. An invisibility potion cannot deceive my friends."

"Th-this is... Wait, a Singer of the Trees?!"

Godwin struggled desperately, but the thin vegetation holding him down may as well have been steel chains.

"Why were you concealing yourself? Did we look like bandits to you?" inquired the high elf woman.

"A-an abundance of caution. It's dangerous to travel alone," Godwin hurriedly replied.

"Even to the point of using a magic potion?"

"I'm a careful man."

"You don't really look it to me."

The high elf was scrutinizing Godwin. Noticing that her coach had stopped, the others in the caravan turned to come back. A cold sweat started pouring down Godwin's back.

"The only place this road leads is the republic of Zoltan, right? Are you from there?"

"Wh-who knows? Hey, I ain't done anything wrong here! And it's not like I can do anything by myself, so just let me go already!"

"I suppose so. I'd appreciate it if you'd answer me just one question, though."

"Wh-what?"

The high elf stooped over, looking straight into Godwin's eyes.

"I've heard there's an adventurer by the name of Rit in Zoltan. Do you know if she associates with a young human man with black hair?

Godwin immediately realized she meant Red.

I've had nothin' but trouble ever since I got involved with him...

Godwin had once confidently thought that he could manage in a fight against most anyone in Zoltan. His encountering Red had blown that notion out of the water, however. Upon reflection,

Godwin realized that was what it meant to be a big frog in a small pond.

But come on! You didn't have go dumping goddamn dragons in the pond! Godwin cursed God for pitting him against such monstrously powerful foes before switching gears back to figuring out how to respond to his captor.

"Did something happen, Ms. Yarandrala?" asked a merchant Godwin had wronged some time ago.

The high elf called Yarandrala, who had once been one of the Hero's comrades, turned to the merchant. Behind him, the road continued into the distance.

And at the end of it lay Zoltan.

Afterword

To everyone who has picked up this book, thank you very much! I'm the author, Zappon.

It's because of your support that this story reached its fourth volume!

When I first envisioned this series, this fourth book was the original conclusion.

Red had been pushed out of the party, Rit never joined the party despite her feelings for Red, and Ruti was forced to be the Hero. The tale of those three finding happiness, starting with Red being kicked out and ending with everyone living happily in the countryside, was the original complete outline. I'm thrilled that I was able to deliver all that to everyone.

The story will continue past that first planned ending, though. The theme of the narrative is a slow life, after all. The details of the actual happily ever after are also an integral part.

What form will Red and Rit's happy days together take? Having finally taken her first steps as an individual, how will Ruti live her new life? I want to write some stories about Tisse and her friend Mister Crawly Wawly, too.

I'll be doing my best to ensure you all enjoy what's to come. Please continue to support Red, Rit, and all of their friends!

At present, I'm starting the draft for the fifth volume. The plan is for the character who showed up at the very end of this book to play an active role.

Speaking of the fifth volume, I have a fantastic announcement. It will come with a special audio-drama CD!

I'll be writing the script for the drama, and the plan is to showcase an ordinary day for Red, Rit, and Ruti with just a bit of adventure dealing with Divine Blessings thrown in.

Since the voice actors will be going through all the effort of giving life to my words, I had to add a little bit of Red and Rit flirting into the script, too. I'm currently struggling with the pleasant problem of imagining what sort of situation would be the most exciting to hear.

That bit will be a special audio recording separate from the main drama. It'll be a scene where Rit sneaks into bed after Red has gone to sleep for the night, and they share a joyous, playful evening. I'm doing my best to illustrate for everyone the sort of happy life Red lives.

The special edition of the fifth volume that contains the audio-drama CD will be a limited run, but if you preorder, you'll be able to reserve a copy, so please do so if you are interested!

I hope you look forward to both the next book and the audio drama.

This fourth volume could not have reached the shelves without the help of many, many people. I would like to take a moment to express my gratitude to them.

To this series editor, Miyakawa, I'm delighted that the work we've created together has managed to continue for this many installments!

To Yasumo, who always provides such lovely illustrations, I feel like there were a few tough drawings this time around. Between the cover, the combat scenes, and the intimate moments, you must have had a rough time. Still, your illustrations are genuinely splendid! Thank you!

To the designer, I'm sorry for constantly asking you to neatly fit such a long series title onto the cover. I owe the cover's appeal all to you!

To the proofreaders, who found so many typos and errors in my drafts, I pale at the thought of those mistakes being in the print book! Thank you for fixing them.

To the folk working to print and bind the actual books, to the people in sales, to those working at the bookstores, and everyone else involved with this book in some way or another, this series could never have reached this point without all your help. Thank you!

And finally, to the readers who picked up this work, whether you have followed this story from the first volume, found this thanks to the manga version, or supported the original online version, this book would not exist without all of you. Thank you so very much!

Next is the fifth volume! There's still more story to tell, so let's meet again!

Zappon
A cloud-filled spring month in 2019

Hello, this is Yasumo. The story was really rousing, and there were several challenging illustrations, but it was fun!

Red reunites with his stalwart friend, Yarandala. But will her return usher in more peaceful days or a terrible disturbance?

BANISHED FROM THE HERO'S PARTY,

I Decided to Live a Quiet Life in the Countryside

5

ON SALE: JANUARY 2022!

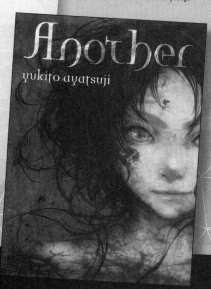